UNDER NEW YORK SKIES

Blame it on the coffee!

An original story by

CONNIE SUAREZ-NISTAL

Ordering Information:

Books to Life Marketing Ltd
128 City Road, London, EC1V 2NX, UK

Printed in the United States of America

Vector graphics by Vecteezy

CONTENTS

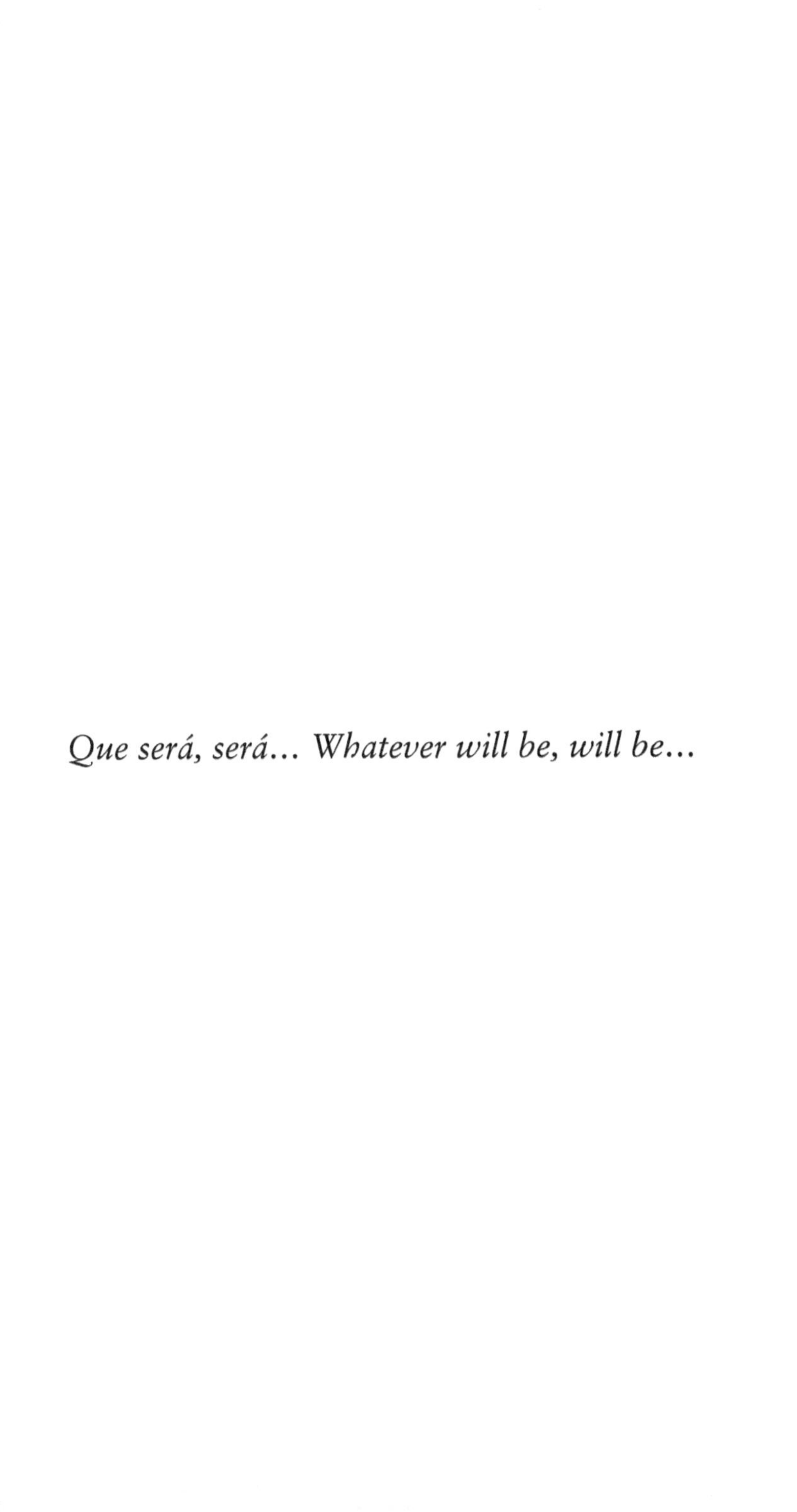

Que será, será... Whatever will be, will be...

JIM

 had just snatched an old lady's handbag in the middle of the street. She barely had time to cry out, her voice trembling with shock:

"Help! I've been robbed!"

The boy sprinted past Jim's patrol car at full speed—right as Jim sat waiting for his partner, who had stepped out for coffee. Instinct took over the moment Jim spotted him. He threw the car door open and launched himself into the chase, leaving the door swinging wide behind him.

The kid ran like a gazelle, weaving between cars as he darted across the street. Jim pushed himself to keep up, raising a hand to signal speeding vehicles to slow down just enough for him to slip through. He was in good shape, but the boy's agility and speed made him feel every year of his age—the kid couldn't have been more than twelve or thirteen.

The chase led straight into a bustling shopping mall, where the dense crowd turned pursuit into a game of reflexes. Jim kept his rhythm, scanning for a glimpse of his target. For a split second, he lost sight of him. Then—there. The boy was heading for the restrooms.

Summoning one last burst of energy, Jim sprinted at full speed, shouting: "Clear the way!"

People stepped aside, some already recognizing him as a cop. But just as he rounded a corner, he collided with a woman carrying a cup of coffee. The impact was unavoidable—the hot liquid splashed across her blouse, with stray droplets landing on Jim's jacket. Instinctively, he grabbed her arm to keep them both from falling, barely managing to steady them both.

"I'm so sorry!" he blurted, pausing just long enough to make sure she was all right before pressing on toward the restrooms. His gut told him the kid was slipping away.

He entered the men's restrooms cautiously. Silence. Everything looked undisturbed. Checking under each stall, he pushed a few doors open— empty. Then, something on the floor caught his eye.

Near one of the sinks lay the elderly woman's handbag.

Jim picked it up and rifled through its contents. As he feared, the wallet—likely containing cash and ID—was gone. No phone, either.

His jaw tightened. He had the bag, but the boy had vanished into thin air.

Jim had to return to where it all began—the spot near his patrol car where the elderly woman had been robbed. He needed to return her handbag and collect some personal details, provided she was in the right state of mind to give them. Filing a report was a priority, but one thing was certain: he had gotten a good look at the kid, and he wouldn't rest until he tracked him down.

As he stepped out of the mall restrooms, still holding the handbag, he noticed the coffee stains on his jacket. The memory of the collision flashed through his mind, and he instinctively scanned the area for the woman. He spotted her quickly— dabbing at her blouse with a damp handkerchief, surrounded by a small group of people who were chatting and laughing light-heartedly about the incident. Deciding he owed her a proper apology; Jim made his way toward them.

Noticing his approach, a few women in the group exchanged amused glances.

"It's that cop!" one of them said with a grin. "Oh, isn't he handsome?" another chimed in. "It's the uniform," joked a third.

Jim acknowledged them with a polite smile. "Ladies," he greeted, then turned his attention to the woman with the coffee stains.

"Are your all right?" he asked.

She kept her head down, still focused on dabbing at her blouse.

"Yes, thank you," she replied quietly.

Jim kept his tone warm. "I'm really sorry about that—I didn't see you"

She shook her head, clearly embarrassed, still avoiding his gaze.

"No, it was my fault. I was distracted… I'm sorry."

Then, finally, she looked up—and for a brief moment, Jim was caught off guard. She wasn't just a young woman; there was something effortlessly captivating about her. A natural beauty, with a quiet sweetness that threw him off balance for half a second. Recovering quickly, he offered her a warm smile.

"At least let me cover the dry-cleaning for your blouse."

She blinked, surprised by the offer.

"Thank you… but it's really not necessary. You were just doing your job. These things happen."

Jim appreciated her understanding. His sharp eye quickly caught the nameplate on her jacket: *Lori Kiloha,* accompanied by the logo of a well-known travel agency. A glance at the group around her—tourists holding cameras and maps—confirmed his assumption. She was a tour guide.

As they spoke, Jim couldn't help but take in the details of Lori's appearance, a habit ingrained by years of training. She was of average height, with dark honey-coloured hair pulled into a high bun. Her striking blue eyes stood out, and the navy-blue trouser suit, paired with a crisp white shirt, gave her a polished yet professional look.

Turning to the group, Jim introduced himself with a polite nod.

"I'm Jim O'Hara. If you ever need anything, don´t hesitate to reach out. Welcome to New York! Hope you're enjoying the city. Just out of curiosity, where are you all from?"

In unison, the group cheerfully responded, "Canada!"

Jim's smile widened. "Beautiful country! I'd love to visit someday."

One of the few men in the group gave a friendly nod.

"Well, if you ever do, you'd be more than welcome, Jim."

Jim appreciated the gesture but turned back to Lori, still determined to insist on covering her dry-cleaning costs.

"Please, I insist," he said firmly.

Lori hesitated, clearly tempted to refuse again, but after a brief pause, she gave him a knowing smile.

After exchanging a few more friendly words, Jim bid them farewell with a polite nod and warm smile, leaving a positive impression.

It wasn't until he turned to go that realization struck him—he had completely forgotten about the elderly woman. His chest tightened as he spun around, hurrying back to the scene of the robbery, her handbag still clutched in his hand.

As he neared the patrol car, relief washed over him. Dimitri, his partner, was already there, sitting on a nearby bench with the woman, speaking in a calm, reassuring tone while taking down her details. He had witnessed the whole thing while returning with their coffees.

When Jim finally arrived with the handbag, the elderly woman's face lit up with gratitude.

Despite her wallet being missing, she immediately tried to offer them a reward.

Jim was quick to wave it off, his tone firm but kind.

"No way, ma'am. You don't owe us a thing—

it's just part of the job." Then, with renewed determination, he added, "I'll find that little rat, and I'll get back every penny, plus all your documents. That's a promise."

Jim and Dimitri spent a little more time reassuring the kind old woman before escorting her to the police station to complete the necessary paperwork. They offered to drive her home afterward, but she declined with a gracious smile.

As it turned out, she was a wealthy widow and quickly called her driver to pick her up. The poor man had been waiting in the mall's parking garage, growing increasingly worried when she hadn't contacted him. When he finally heard the full story, he sighed in relief, grateful that his employer was unharmed.

"Don't worry, Mrs. Farrell," Dimitri said, addressing her by name after gathering her details. "We'll recover everything they stole. You have our word."

Mrs. Farrell was visibly touched and insisted on compensating both officers for their kindness.

But Jim and Dimitri politely declined, instead apologizing for the incident occurring under their watch, feeling a sense of responsibility for not preventing it.

For Jim, this case felt strangely personal. Something about Mrs. Farrell reminded him of his late grandmother, Leonora—a warm and inspiring presence from his childhood. That resemblance stirred a deep sense of protectiveness in him, further fuelling his determination to track down the thief.

The following morning, sanitation workers stumbled upon an unexpected find—a woman's wallet discarded in a garbage bin. Inside, they discovered an ID belonging to Mrs. Agatha Farrell, though the cash was missing. Following protocol, they turned it over to the police, where some officers immediately recognized the name and alerted Jim and Dimitri, who were leading the investigation.

Further analysis of the wallet revealed fingerprints, offering a glimmer of hope in identifying the thief. However, when the results came back, they were inconclusive—the boy's prints weren't in the system. No criminal record.

It was probably his first offense.

And Jim was determined to make sure it didn't become the first of many.

After tracking down Mrs. Farrell's address, Jim and Dimitri decided to return the wallet to her in person.

When they arrived at her home, they handed it back with a sincere apology for not having recovered the missing cash—or her mobile phone, which was still unaccounted for.

Far from being upset, the elderly woman accepted the wallet with a warm smile, her gratitude evident.

"Thank you, officers. Truly. The money… well, that's gone, and I can live with that." She sighed, resigned to the reality of the situation. "But this wallet—it means the world to me. My late husband gave it to me years ago, and losing it would've hurt far more than the money ever could."

Jim and Dimitri exchanged a knowing glance. They had seen first-hand how sentimental value often outweighed monetary loss.

She then expressed another concern—the missing phone. More than just a device, it contained personal data and irreplaceable family contacts. "I just hate the thought of someone going through my things," she admitted.

Understanding her distress, Jim reassured her, "We'll do everything we can to find it, ma'am. That's a promise."

Wanting to show her appreciation, Mrs. Farrell offered them coffee or something to drink. Though tempted, Jim and Dimitri politely declined, explaining with a smile that they were still on duty.

As they left, they couldn't help but feel a quiet satisfaction. They had returned more than just a wallet—they had restored a piece of her peace of mind. And though the case wasn't closed yet, they were more determined than ever to track down the missing phone.

When Jim was twenty-six and just starting out as a rookie recruit, Dimitri Papadakis was his instructor. Back then, Dimitri had a reputation for being strict but fair—qualities that quickly earned Jim's respect. His experience, no-nonsense teaching style, and unwavering integrity left a lasting impression.

Over the years, Jim worked with various partners—some exceptional, others less so. But fate eventually brought him back to Dimitri, no longer as his mentor but as his partner. By then, Jim was thirty years old and Dimitri forty-six.

Now, after nearly eleven years of working side by side, they know each other inside and out. They've become an efficient, tightly knit team where trust and understanding are second nature. More than just colleagues, they're close friends. Dimitri, whose roots trace back to Greece, has been a guiding figure for Jim—almost like an older brother. He taught Jim not just how to be a good cop, but how to navigate life's challenges with wisdom and resilience.

Dimitri has been married for years and takes immense pride in his large, loving family. He often nudges Jim with a knowing smile:

"You should find yourself a good girl, settle down, and start a family. You have no idea what you're missing."

But Jim, ever the sceptic, always shrugs it off with a casual reply:

"There aren't any decent girls left, Dimitri. I'm better off single, believe me."

Despite Dimitri's good-natured persistence, Jim isn't in a rush. He's content with his life— focused on his career, enjoying the freedom of bachelorhood. But deep down, he isn't opposed to settling down. The truth is, Jim is simply wait-ing for the right woman. Beneath his practical mindset lies a man who values family, love, and commitment more than he cares to admit.

James O'Hara—known to everyone as Jim—is the eldest son of Conor O'Hara, an Irish firefighter, and Selena Smith, a public relations professional from London. His parents' love story began at a wedding in London, where Conor, the best friend of the groom's brother, met Selena, one of the bridesmaids. At the time, Conor was twenty-five, and Selena was nineteen.

Conor had left his native Ireland at nineteen, seeking new opportunities in London. He worked a series of odd jobs—delivering packages, washing windows, and working as a hotel bellboy—before finally achieving his dream of becoming a fire-fighter after passing the gruelling entrance exams. Selena, meanwhile, was dedicated to her studies in Public Relations.

Their romance was intense and enduring. Two and a half years after they met, they married in London. By the time their first child, James, was born, Conor was twenty-nine and Selena twenty-four. Though motherhood brought new challenges, Selena found a way to balance her career with raising their son.

It was around this time that Conor's cousins in New York told him about the wealth of opportunities in the U.S., particularly for an experienced firefighter like him. While their life in London was comfortable, the couple felt ready for a change. After much consideration, they made the bold decision to move to New York, reasoning that with only one young child, the transition would be manageable. And if things didn't work out, they could always return home.

Packing up their essentials, they set out for a fresh start. Conor quickly secured a position with the Fire Department, while Selena landed a job as a public relations specialist at a prestigious hotel. Soon after, five-year-old Jim started elementary school.

Just over a year after settling in, their family grew with the arrival of a baby girl, Nicholle—affectionately called Nicky. Wanting to prioritize her growing family, Selena scaled back her work hours, dedicating more time to raising her children.

Jim and Nicky grew up in a home filled with love, discipline, and strong values. To Selena's surprise, Nicky developed a rebellious streak and was something of a tomboy—quite the opposite of the refined, elegant young lady her mother had imagined, and longed for. Jim, on the other hand, was quiet and well-behaved. Though his grades were average, he only excelled in the subjects that truly captured his interest.

When Jim graduated from high school, he was still uncertain about his future. His parents encouraged him to attend university, but he had yet to discover his true calling and wasn't sure what to study. Unconvinced about following in his father's footsteps as a firefighter, he chose to enrol in Architecture—a field he found interesting, even if he wasn't entirely sure it was the right fit.

At nineteen, while Jim was in his first year of university and Nicky was thirteen, the family received unexpected news: Selena, at forty-three, was pregnant. The surprise was immense—they had assumed their parenting years were behind them. Nine months later, the O'Hara family welcomed its newest member: Andrew.

Andy quickly became the heart of the household, adored, and doted on by everyone. With their years of experience and financial stability, Conor and Selena embraced this new chapter of parenthood with ease, while Jim and Nicky—now teenagers—showered their little brother with affection. Andy grew up in a home filled with love, becoming the cherished link that strengthened the family's already deep bond. Despite their differences in personality, Jim, Nicky, and Andy—the only one to follow in his father's footsteps as a firefighter—form a peculiar yet inseparable trio, reflecting the warm and resilient spirit of the O'Hara family.

Jim shares a particularly strong connection with Andy, and it's no surprise—he has always had a soft spot for children, and with the significant age gap between them, Jim feels more like a father that a brother to Andy. Before Andy's arrival, Nicky had been "the apple of Jim's eye," and though she still holds a special place in his heart, the youngest O'Hara now also occupies a cherished spot. As the eldest sibling, Jim naturally became their confidant—Nicky and Andy, both trust him with secrets they wouldn't dare share with their parents. His wisdom, experience, and steady nature make him not only a protective older brother but also a trusted advisor and lifelong friend.

After five long years of studying Architecture, Jim was on the verge of graduating when someone mentioned the Police Academy to him. The idea intrigued him, prompting him to learn more. The application process wasn't easy—there were extensive paperwork requirements, a rigorous medical exam, and a thorough background check—but Jim passed each stage effortlessly, thanks to his spotless record. Shortly after earning his degree in Architecture, he enrolled in the New York Police Academy, where he discovered his true passion.

What had started as mere curiosity quickly became a commitment. Jim excelled as a cadet, embracing every challenge and thriving in the structured, high-intensity environment. Before long, he realized he had found his true calling.

Beyond his dedication to his career, Jim is a deeply family-oriented and affectionate man. He cherishes lively gatherings around a table full of food, conversations filled with laughter, and celebrations where the whole family comes together. While he isn't in a rush, he dreams of starting his own family someday—ideally with several children. However, he knows that finding someone who shares his vision isn't easy. He's had a few relationships, but many women have called him "old fashioned." The truth is, while Jim has a modern mind-set, he holds onto values and courtesies he considers essential—principles instilled in him at home, which set him apart.

He's not particularly drawn to fleeting trends like tattoos, piercings, extravagant hairstyles, or flashy clothing. His style is classic and pragmatic. As a teenager, he briefly experimented with smoking but quickly decided it wasn't for him. He has always steered clear of drugs and other harmful habits—an outlook that his work in law enforcement has only reinforced.

That said, Jim isn't without his vices. His biggest weakness—his true addiction—is coffee. Without his morning cup, he's sluggish and unfocused until the caffeine kicks in. Throughout the day, coffee remains his faithful companion, and if he can pair it with a donut, even better. He also enjoys a good drink now and then, particularly beer, but always in moderation.

Style-wise, Jim prefers a timeless look. His everyday wardrobe consists of jeans, t-shirts, and shorts in the summer, though he has no hesitation about dressing in a suit and tie when the occasion calls for it. He sometimes wears caps but avoids earrings or other accessories, keeping his style simple and clean. His hair is always short and well-groomed, reflecting his practical and polished nature.

Physically, Jim has a presence that's hard to overlook. Standing at an above-average height with a balanced, athletic build, he possesses striking features inherited from his father—deep blue eyes and dark hair. While he typically prefers a clean-shaven look, he occasionally experiments with a moustache or a neatly trimmed beard, always maintaining a refined appearance. His understated confidence and classic style make him an attractive figure, both in and out of uniform.

Currently, Jim lives in a small apartment in the heart of Manhattan, a location that perfectly suits his lifestyle, work, and independence. However, until recently, he shared the family apartment with his siblings. The O'Hara home, filled with childhood memories, remains close by, allowing them to maintain their deep-rooted connection.

The apartment had always been the heart of the O'Hara family—a place filled with warmth and history. When Conor and Selena retired, they decided to move to a quiet suburban neighbourhood, leaving the apartment to their children. Not only was it a cherished space, but its central location made it convenient for them to stay connected to the city while enjoying their independence.

Though Jim enjoys the freedom of his own place, he still feels a deep attachment to his childhood home. He regularly meets up with his siblings there, sharing dinners, laughter, and reminiscing about old times. Some nights, nostalgia or sheer comfort compels him to stay over, making him feel as though he never truly left.

Andy, the youngest, spends the most time at the family apartment, while Nicky, due to her military career, is often stationed in Virginia, returning home only when on leave. When she's back, the apartment once again comes alive with the energy of the O'Hara siblings—rekindling the essence of their shared past.

On special occasions—Christmas, Thanksgiving, Easter, and birthdays—the entire family gathers at their parents' house, where tradition and love continue to bind them together, proving that no matter where life takes them, home will always be where the O'Haras are.

ST. PATRICK'S DAY

 in New York is celebrated with the same fervour as in Ireland itself, as the entire city bursts into a sea of green festivities. The Irish, who make up a significant part of the population, proudly honour their roots, while grand parades march down the city's most iconic avenues. Locals and visitors alike crowd the streets, eager to be part of the celebration.

Amidst the revelry, Jim and Dimitri are on patrol, working to maintain order in the chaos of noise and excitement. The dense crowd jostles them as people squeeze through the streets, trying to get a better view of the parade. They stay vigilant, ensuring lost children are quickly reunited with their families and preventing anyone from getting carried away in the festive frenzy.

The packed streets also create the perfect hunting ground for pickpockets, who take advantage of every distraction. Jim and Dimitri remain on high alert, their eyes scanning every corner to keep the celebration safe and incident-free. It's a challenging task, but they're used to managing crowds and striking a balance between security and the spirited energy of the day.

As they monitor the area, a young woman approaches them with a worried expression.

Behind her, a small group follows closely, each wearing a yellow flag pinned to their lapel—except for her. She clutches a larger flag in her hand, as if wanting to be easily seen.

Jim, ever observant, recognizes her face even before she speaks. She looks familiar, and in an instant, his mind makes the connection.

"The girl with the spilled coffee..."

A faint smile flickers across his face just as she begins to speak.

"Officer..." she starts urgently, but then hesitates, her expression shifting as recognition dawns on her.

"Oh... hello. Sorry to bother you," she corrects herself, still visibly uneasy.

"No problem," Jim responds, straightening slightly, his attention sharpening.

"I think I've lost one of my tourists," she explains, but before she can elaborate, an older woman beside her steps forward. Her voice trembles, and her eyes glisten with unshed tears.

"It's my husband…" she stammers, barely holding back her distress. "He went into the mall's bathroom a while ago… and he hasn't come back. I haven't heard from him. We were supposed to meet at twelve to rejoin the group, but he never showed up."

"Don't worry, ma'am," Dimitri said reassuringly. "Can you tell me your husband's name and what he's wearing? Any other details that might help us identify him?"

The woman took a steadying breath, trying to contain her nerves. "His name is Dan," she replied. "He's wearing grey pants, a blue plaid shirt, and a blue jacket. He also has a hearing aid—he has trouble hearing," she added, her voice trembling slightly.

Jim gave a firm nod, committing the description to memory. Every detail could be crucial.

Without wasting a second, he and Dimitri exchanged a glance and set off toward the mall. Moving swiftly, they headed straight for the men's restroom—the last place Dan had been seen.

Dimitri stepped inside to check, while Jim scanned the surrounding area. He carefully searched the hallways, paying special attention to the souvenir stalls, in case Dan had gotten distracted by something along the way.

And there he was.

Standing inside a small souvenir shop, flipping through postcards, was a man matching the exact description: grey pants, blue plaid shirt, blue jacket—and a small yellow flag pinned to his lapel. He appeared completely absorbed, oblivious to the concern he had caused.

Jim approached and tapped him lightly on the shoulder. "Dan?"

The man turned, blinking in surprise.

Indeed, it was the missing tourist. He had simply lost track of time, unaware of the stir his absence had caused—especially for his wife and Lori, the group leader, whose concern had quickly escalated into fear that something serious had happened.

Dan, however, remained blissfully unaware. With an amused smile, he glanced at everyone and said, "All this fuss for me? I'm flattered."

His wife, clearly unimpressed, shot him a sharp look before exclaiming with exasperation,

"You're worse than a child! I can't leave you alone for a second without your wandering off."

Dan chuckled, raising his hands in surrender. "I lost track of time, sweetheart, I admit it. I'm really sorry... I didn't mean to scare you." He turned to the others and added with a sheepish grin, "Sorry, sorry, sorry."

His playful apology earned a round of relieved laughter from the group. The tension melted away, and with a collective sigh, they all realized—thankfully—this had been nothing more than a harmless scare.

Jim couldn't help but notice that the tourists' accents sounded familiar. Driven by curiosity, he stepped closer and, with a friendly smile, asked where they were from.

"Southern Ireland!" they responded in unison, their voices carrying unmistakable warmth.

A grin spread across Jim's face. "My father's Irish," he said proudly, his connection to his roots shining through.

The coincidence sparked excitement within the group. Conversations bubbled up as they eagerly asked about his father's hometown and his heritage. The atmosphere shifted, growing warmer—almost as if a newfound camaraderie had formed between them.

After sincerely thanking the officers for their help. Lori took a quick headcount, calling out names one by one until she confirmed that everyone was present.

When she finished, she turned to Jim, who, along with Dimitri, had lingered to ensure they weren't needed any longer.

Jim met Lori's gaze with an open, friendly smile. Nearby, Dimitri watched the exchange with amusement. He didn't miss the subtle glances passing between them, and with a knowing smirk, he sensed there was something more than simple cordiality in the air.

Finally, Lori turned back to her group, her voice brimming with energy.

"While we wait for the coach to take us to that promised surprise lunch spot, why don't we find a great place to watch the parade?" she suggested, her enthusiasm contagious. Then, with a playful glint in her eyes, she added, "And please—no one else wander off!"

Jim and Dimitri helped clear a space for them, a small but appreciated gesture that earned more grateful smiles. The tourists gathered excitedly, settling in to enjoy the spectacle unfolding before them.

"I hope you're all hungry!" Lori exclaimed, her excitement growing. She had something truly special planned—an exclusive St. Patrick's Day feast at an authentic Irish restaurant in the heart of Manhattan.

Even though the group hailed from Ireland, Lori had carefully crafted an experience that would make them feel at home while embracing the vibrant energy of New York. It was a fusion of tradition and adventure, a chance to celebrate their culture in a city that welcomed it with open arms.

After finishing their duties and bidding the group farewell with well wishes for their stay in New York, Dimitri turned to Jim with a mischievous smirk. Letting out a low chuckle, he teased:

"Come on, Casanova, let's get back to work."

Jim, still amused by the exchange, raised an eyebrow and shot back with mock indignation, "Casanova? Me? I think you've got the wrong movie, Dimitri."

They shared a knowing glance, their easy camaraderie evident. Jokes aside, the day was far from over, and there was still work to be done. Without further delay, they resumed their patrol, though a subtle sense of relief and lingering amusement softened the usual weight of duty.

Yet, as Jim walked the familiar streets, his thoughts kept circling back to the friendly tour guide. He wasn't sure why, but something about Lori had stuck with him—her energy, her smile, the way she had effortlessly commanded the group's attention.

Tourist groups had always been part of the city's daily chaos, blending into the background of his routine. But now, for the first time, he found himself noticing them. Catching glimpses of tour guides in the crowd, his gaze lingered a little longer.

Was she there?

Without meaning to, he began scanning the city differently—crowded sidewalks, bustling cafés, even the busy shopping districts. A part of him was waiting, watching, wondering if fate might arrange another unexpected encounter.

And for reasons he wasn't quite ready to admit, the thought didn't seem so bad.

It was a rainy morning when Jim stepped out to grab coffee. He made his way to one of the usual spots, a coffee shop where he and Dimitri were already well-known. As expected, there was a small line, but he didn't mind. He placed the order—two coffees, one for himself and one for Dimitri—and, on a whim, added a couple of donuts.

As he approached the counter to pick up his order, he casually glanced at the growing line—and then he saw her.

Lori.

Their eyes met, and for a brief second, surprise flickered between them before settling into warm smiles.

"Good morning!" Jim greeted, still slightly caught off guard to see her there, especially this early. He tilted his head playfully. "Didn't take you for an early bird."

"Morning," Lori replied, returning his smile. "I need my coffee fix before wrangling my little herd of tourists."

Her gaze drifted to the tray he was balancing, her curiosity piqued by the donuts.

"Which one do you recommend?" she asked, nodding toward them.

Jim grinned. "The one with rainbow sprin-kles—trust me, life-changing."

Lori smirked, considering her options. "Mmm, sounds tempting."

Jim adjusted his grip on the tray, glancing toward the door. "Well, duty calls. My partner's waiting. Hope to see you again—and seriously, try the donut. You won't regret it." His confident smile lingered just a moment longer than necessary.

"I'll take your word for it," Lori said, her eyes gleaming with amusement.

With a small nod, Jim turned and stepped back out into the misty morning, leaving behind the warm, coffee-scented air of the shop. But as he walked away, something felt different.

That brief encounter had left an unexpected spark in its wake—something light, almost electric. He wasn't sure why, but his steps felt a little lighter, his mood just a little brighter. It was ridiculous, really. It was just a conversation. A few words. A donut recommendation.

And yet…

By the time he returned to Dimitri, his partner had already picked up on the shift in his demeanour.

Dimitri arched an eyebrow, eyeing Jim's lingering smile with amusement.

"And that grin?" he mused, crossing his arms. "You look like you just won the lottery."

As they settled into the patrol car, parked right in front of the coffee shop where Jim had picked up their order, they prepared to enjoy their breakfast. Just as Jim reached for his coffee, the shop door swung open.

Lori stepped outside, coffee in one hand, a donut in the other.

Dimitri spotted her instantly—and just as quickly, he caught the reason behind Jim's slightly dazed expression.

"Huh," Dimitri mused, a slow, knowing grin spreading across his face. "Now *that's* better than winning the lottery."

Without missing a beat, he started humming *Love Is in the Air,* his tone deliberately exaggerated, turning the moment into pure mischief.

Jim shot him a look, but the traitorous warmth creeping up his neck gave him away. He could *feel* the faint blush, no matter how hard he tried to will it away.

"Really?" he muttered, shaking his head as he sipped his coffee.

But Dimitri only smirked, eyes gleaming with amusement.

Jim sighed, but the truth was—he couldn't stop smiling either. And as much as he wasn't ready to *define* whatever this was, one thing was certain: the thought of Lori had left a mark, one he wasn't quite ready to shake off just yet.

One afternoon, as they patrolled the streets, Jim drove the squad car, eyes scanning the sidewalks out of habit. Dimitri, seated beside him, was reviewing a list of pending reports when they stopped at a red light.

That's when Jim's gaze locked onto a figure in the crowd.

Something about the person tugged at his memory. He frowned, narrowing his eyes, focusing. A few seconds later, his expression hardened.

Without a word, he flung the car door open and bolted.

Dimitri barely had time to react before Jim was already sprinting down the sidewalk.

His target? The young pickpocket—the same one who had snatched Agatha Farrell's wallet last time.

For a moment, the kid remained blissfully unaware, strolling along as if he had all the time in the world. Then, out of the corner of his eye, he spotted Jim barrelling towards him.

Panic flashed across his face. He turned on his heels and ran. But he never stood a chance.

Jim closed the distance in seconds, grabbing the boy's arm in a firm, unshakable grip.

"Gotcha, kid," he said, a satisfied smirk tugging at the corner of his lips. "Let's take a little walk—to the station."

The boy twisted, kicked, fought with everything he had. But Jim had seen it all before. He barely budged.

"Let me go! I didn't do anything!" the kid protested, his voice laced with false innocence.

Jim let out a dry, amused chuckle. "Yeah, sure. And I'm a blind man."

Without wasting another second, Jim cuffed the boy and led him to the patrol car, where Dimitri was already behind the wheel. The kid didn't stop squirming, spitting out protests, curses, and expletives.

"Hey, hey! Watch your mouth, kid!" Dimitri called out, raising an eyebrow as he glanced at the rearview mirror.

A few minutes later, Dimitri eyed the boy through the mirror and asked, "What's your name, son?"

"Luke Skywalker," the boy shot back, shamelessly.

Dimitri and Jim exchanged a knowing look, both trying to hide their smiles.

Back at the station, as the arrest was being processed, the officers searched the boy. They found three mobile phones in his pockets. After cross-checking the serial numbers, they confirmed that all three had been reported as stolen. One of them belonged to Mrs. Farrell, the elderly woman who had been the victim of the robbery.

Following protocol, they began contacting the rightful owners to arrange the return of the devices.

As they dug deeper into the boy's background, his real identity was revealed: Daniel Finch, a teenager with a history of foster care, multiple escapes from various homes, and a string of minor thefts. Though his offenses hadn't been serious enough to form a criminal record, his escalating behaviour was a concern. The theft of Mrs. Farrell's wallet marked a worrying shift in his conduct.

Jim, wanting to understand the motivations behind the boy's actions, decided to have a word with him. They had left him in the interrogation room to cool off for a bit.

After learning everything they could about Daniel, Jim and Dimitri returned to the room. Jim held a bottle of water in one hand and placed it on the table as he stood, arms crossed, his expression firm.

Before Jim could speak, the boy sneered and broke the silence.

"Is that water so you can get my fingerprints and DNA?" he asked, his voice dripping with sarcasm and mock suspicion.

Jim raised an eyebrow, his lips curling into a small smile. "Could be," he replied coolly, shrugging.

The boy smirked, as if he thought he had outsmarted them.

"Well, I'm not touching it or drinking anything," he declared, crossing his arms in defiance.

Jim gave a casual shrug. "Suit yourself," he said, his tone neutral, letting the silence build tension.

Daniel's frown deepened as he weighed his options. Despite his bravado, the dry feeling in his mouth and the weariness creeping into his body were undeniable. But giving in would mean losing his edge, wouldn't it?

Jim, for his part, knew it was only a matter of time before the kid cracked.

"Alright, ... Danny..." Jim began, deliberately stressing the boy's real name to remind him that they weren't fooled.

"Let's skip the theatrics. What did you do with the money from the wallet?" Jim's voice was firm, his eyes locked on the boy, trying to instil some fear.

The boy shrugged nonchalantly, feigning indifference.

"What money? There wasn't any—"

Jim slammed his knuckles on the table, cutting him off. "Don't play me for a fool. We both know there was a considerable amount in that wallet. So, cut the crap."

The boy hesitated, swallowed hard, then exploded in frustration. "Fine! I spent it, okay, dude? Happy now?"

Jim exhaled with exaggerated patience, placing his hands on his hips. "Well, now you're gonna have to earn it back."

The boy raised an eyebrow, letting out a mocking laugh. "Are you crazy? How do you expect me to do that? I already told you, dude—I spent it."

Jim flashed a crooked smile. "Community service until the debt's paid off," he said sarcastically. Then, mimicking the boy's tone, he added, "...dude."

The boy stared at him, incredulous, but Jim wasn't finished.

"And not only that..." Jim leaned forward slightly, his voice lowering in a more serious tone.

"When you've worked off every last penny, I'll personally take you to Mrs. Farrell's house, and you'll hand it over to her. Oh, and don't forget the best part—you'll apologize to her. Got it?" He watched the boy closely, searching for any flicker of remorse.

The boy held his gaze defiantly, like he was testing Jim's authority. But after a few seconds of tense silence, he lowered his head with a frustrated grunt, saying nothing.

Jim exchanged a look with Dimitri, who had been observing the entire interaction, arms crossed. It was clear: the boy wasn't ready to show any real remorse yet, but maybe, just maybe, this could be the opportunity to help him turn things around.

Jim made the decision to personally return Mrs. Farrell's phone, and Dimitri accompanied him. They wanted to do more than just return the phone—they wanted to explain the boy's punishment and reassure Mrs. Farrell that her loss would be fully paid back.

When they arrived, Jim pulled an envelope from his jacket and handed it to her with a warm smile.

"We recovered your phone," he said softly, "and it seems to be intact."

Mrs. Farrell took the envelope with trembling hands, opened it carefully, and pulled out the phone. Her face softened with relief, her eyes lighting up.

"What a joy!" she exclaimed, her voice cracking slightly. "You don't know how much this means to me. All my contacts, my important things... Thank you, really."

Jim and Dimitri shared a look, a quiet acknowledgment that they had done their part. Giving her peace of mind was all that mattered now.

However, when Jim explained what had been done with the boy, her expression shifted.

"Thank you for your efficiency. You both deserve a promotion." she said with a light laugh, but then sighed, her tone softening. "But... let's allow the boy to follow his own path. I hope he's learned his lesson. Money isn't the most important thing... what matters is remorse. I hope this is a turning point for him."

As she always did, Mrs. Farrell offered them a warm drink before they left. But with grateful smiles, they declined. They still had patrols to finish, after all.

They exchanged goodbyes, and as they stepped back into the street, Mrs. Farrell watched them with a kind, thankful expression, her heart eased just a little by the return of what mattered most to her.

HOSTAGE

IT WAS JUST another routine patrol when Jim notices the arrival of a large tour bus pulling up to the curb. One by one, the passengers began to step off—probably eager tourists ready to start their walking tour and pick up some souvenirs.

Dimitri, always attentive to small details, quickly picked up on how his partner kept his eyes fixed on the vehicle, as if expecting to see someone in particular. With a mischievous grin, he couldn't resist teasing him.

"See something that interests you?" he asked playfully. "And what if it's not her?"

Jim clicked his tongue, trying to hide his anticipation, but the sparkle in his eyes gave him away. He couldn't help but wonder if, among the tourists stepping off, he would spot the cheerful guide who had been occupying more space in his mind lately than he was willing to admit.

Dimitri let out a chuckle, crossing his arms as he observed his friend with an amused look.

"Well, Jim… I've never seen you this interested in local tourism."

Jim rolled his eyes and turned away from the bus with feigned indifference, but the faint flush on his cheeks did not go unnoticed by his partner.

To his pleasant surprise, the last one to step off was her… Lori!

Jim felt a slight flutter in his stomach at the sight of her. From the very first day he saw her, he had taken note of the name tag on her jacket, which displayed her name along with the company she worked for. That's why, the moment he recognized the logo on the tour bus, he knew his hunch had been right.

Beside him, Dimitri wasted no time in seizing the opportunity to have some fun at his expense. With a smug grin and arms crossed, he gave him a light nudge.

"And there she is! Enjoy the view while you can…" he teased with satisfaction.

Jim let out a sigh, trying to keep his composure, but Dimitri wasn't done yet.

"Well, what are you waiting for? Why don't you go say hi? Don't be shy." He laughed and added in an even more mischievous tone, "Come on, Jim, it's not every day you have a legitimate excuse to approach your 'tourist muse'."

Jim shot him a warning glance, but he couldn't stop a small smile from creeping onto his lips. For a brief moment, he considered the idea… and his heart beat just a little faster.

While Dimitri insisted that Jim should at least go say hello, he assured him that he would wait by the patrol car, enjoying the show.

Jim let out a sigh, then decided to go along with it. He crossed the road, raising his hand to signal a couple of speeding cars, forcing them to slow down as he moved through the traffic.

Before he even reached the bus, Lori had already spotted him coming. Her eyes lit up in recognition, and as he got closer, a wide, genuine smile spread across her face.

For a moment, they were completely absorbed in each other, oblivious to everything else. Her new group of tourists watched them with amused smiles, some even exchanging knowing glances, clearly captivated by the undeniable connection between them. Amid the murmurs, a few seemed to assume they were a couple, as if their closeness and natural chemistry were obvious enough to give that impression.

But then, in an instant, everything changed.

A sharp, deafening sound cut through the murmurs—gunshots!

Jim, who was still short of the sidewalk, reacted instinctively. He crouched slightly, his hand immediately going to his gun. Dimitri, already on high alert, reached for his weapon and began crossing the street, moving swiftly toward his partner.

The group of tourists panicked, their murmurs turning anxious. Lori, maintaining her composure, quickly turned to them and, in a firm yet calm voice, instructed:

"Get back on the bus and stay low in your seats. We don't know what's happening yet. It's probably just a false alarm or a firecracker, but it's best to be cautious. Stay calm."

As the tourists obeyed and hurried back inside, she remained by the bus door, ensuring everyone was safe.

Jim moved quickly, his eyes locked on Lori and the bus. His instincts screaming at him to hurry, but before he could reach her, a hooded man suddenly appeared.

Only his eyes, blazing with fury, and his mouth, twisted by incoherent screams, were visible. Holding a gun in his hand, he fired into the air again and again, spreading panic through the crowd.

In an instant, everything changed.

Before Jim could react, the man lunged at Lori, grabbing her forcefully and taking her hostage.

The situation had just become far more dangerous.

Practically dragging Lori to a corner, he held her in a tight grip. His ragged breathing betrayed his nervousness.

"Don't come any closer, or I'll kill her!" he shouted, his voice wavering between rage and fear.

Jim raised both hands in a placating gesture.

Every word mattered.

"Let her go, and we'll talk calmly," he said in a steady voice, making no sudden movements, careful not to agitate him further.

But the man shook his head frantically, his eyes wild.

"No! If I let her go, they'll kill me."

Jim studied him closely. His eyes reflected the anguish of a desperate man, his rigid stance on the verge of collapse. But it wasn't just desperation—fear and confusion swirled in his gaze. Something didn't add up.

Meanwhile, Dimitri had already called for reinforcements over the radio. They arrived quickly. Within seconds, the street filled with patrol cars, flashing lights, and officers with their weapons drawn, all aimed at the suspect.

The police chief arrived, and Dimitri swiftly briefed him on the situation. The superior nodded before issuing a firm order:

"No one fires until I give the command!"

The officers took their positions behind the vehicles, ready to act, their sights locked on the man holding Lori hostage.

Despite, the danger, Lori fought to remain calm. She could feel the cold barrel pressing against her temple, every tremor in the man's grip a chilling reminder of how close she was to death. His unsteady finger hovered over the trigger—one wrong move, and it would be all over. Lori held her breath, forcing herself not to dwell on it.

Meanwhile, Jim took a subtle step forward, keeping his voice firm yet soothing.

"Listen, what's going on?" he asked gently, searching for a way to connect. "You don't want to hurt anyone, right? Tell us what you need, we'll help you. Just let her go."

The man blinked several times; his grip on Lori wavered slightly. For the first time, he seemed unsure.

Jim seized the moment...

"Tell me your name," he pressed, his voice just as calm. "Help me understand what's happening to you."

The air was thick with tension. Every passing second was a dangerous game between desperation and the possibility of a peaceful resolution.

"Jack," the man muttered after a brief pause, his voice tight. Probably a fake name, but it would do for now. He tightened his grip on Lori and pressed the gun's barrel harder against her temple.

"All right, Jack. I'm Jim," the agent responded, his tone calm but firm. "Listen, why don't you let her go? She hasn't done anything to you."

Jack didn't answer right away. His breathing was erratic, his gaze darting around, searching for an escape he couldn't find.

Jim took another step forward, keeping his hands clearly visible.

"Don't come any closer!" Jack shouted, his voice breaking between panic and rage.

"Alright... I won't move. But let her go, and we'll talk," Jim insisted, carefully measuring each word. "I promise we'll listen to you. Something is wrong, isn't it? Otherwise, you wouldn't be here."

Jack clenched his jaw and shook his head frantically.

"No! I won't let her go until someone listens to me! No one ever listens! No one cares!"

With a rough motion, he presses the gun even harder against Lori's temple. She held her breath, biting her lips to keep from letting out a sound.

Jack trembled. For an instant, his eyes revealed something beyond anger—a shadow of fear. But his desperation still controlled him.

They were standing right beside a glass door leading into a laundromat. Inside, customers and employees watched the scene unfold with terrified expressions. Realizing the danger, a few employees remembered the back door near the restrooms, which led to a side alley. Quietly, they motioned for people to start slipping out one by one without making a sound.

Suddenly, Jack shoved the door open with his back, forcing Lori inside with him. The jingle of the entry bell clashed starkly with the brutality of the moment.

Once inside, he turned the lock, barricading the main entrance.

At that moment, a sharp noise echoed from the back of the shop—the rear door had just shut. Jack's head snapped toward the sound, his nerves on edge. Still holding onto Lori, he dragged her toward the back of the laundromat. With a forceful shove, he blocked the rear exit as well, eliminating any chance of escape.

He returned to the front of the laundromat, holding her with one hand while pressing the gun firmly against her temple with the other.

The danger escalated with every passing second, and time was working against them.

Jim felt a knot of frustration, helplessness, and rage tightening in his stomach as he watched Jack barricade himself inside with Lori as his hostage. He had been so close... and yet, he had let him slip into the building.

Desperate, he searched Dimitri's gaze for answers.

His partner, always the calmer of the two, placed a firm hand on his shoulder.

"Jim, we're getting her out of there," he assured him, his voice deep and resolute. "I promise you."

Jim exhaled sharply, forcing himself to stay level-headed. He couldn't lose control now.

Just a few meters away, the police chief analysed the situation, his brow furrowed. Wasting no time, he began issuing orders over the radio.

"I want two units in the back alley. Find a way in without alerting him. If we can get her out without violence, we will."

Then, he pointed to a specialized officer.

"Get up to the roof of that low building. I need a sniper with a clear view of the target."

The marksman nodded and immediately set off.

"Nobody fires unless I give the order," the chief warned in a stern tone. "We don't want to kill him, but if this spirals out of control, we won't have a choice."

Jim heard that last part with a tight knot in his chest. If Jack didn't back down… if things escalated… there might be no other way.

But he couldn't let it come to that. Not while there was still a chance to prevent it.

Every second mattered. If Jack became any more agitated, Lori would be in real danger. He couldn't just stand by and wait for the situation to resolve itself by force. He had to talk to him before it was too late.

Taking a deep breath, he made a desperate decision.

"I'm going in," Jim announced firmly. Dimitri grabbed his arm instantly.

"Have you lost your mind? If you go in there without a plan, you could make things worse."

Jim met his gaze with determination, his voice steady but filled with urgency.

"I have to talk to him. We can still prevent this from ending in tragedy. Jack isn't just a common criminal—he's desperate, scared. If we corner him any further, he might make a decision he can't take back."

The police chief stood with his arms crossed, assessing the situation.

"It's too risky," he growled. "But... what exactly are you thinking?"

Jim looked toward the laundromat. He knew that if he could get Jack to see him as an ally rather than a threat, they might have a chance.

"I want to go in unarmed," he proposed. "I'll leave my gun here. If he thinks I'm not a danger to him, maybe he'll tell me what's going on and what he wants."

Dimitri stared at him as if he had lost his mind.

"That's suicide, Jim. What if he doesn't listen to you?"

"Do you have a better plan?" Jim shot back. "If I go in armed, he'll feel cornered and react badly. But if he sees me unarmed, if I talk to him like a human being instead of a cop trying to take him down, he might hesitate—just for a second. And that's when I'll have a chance to disarm him."

The police chief frowned, studying him carefully.

"And if your plan fails?… I don't like this."

Jim exhaled in frustration, feeling the weight of time pressing down on him.

"Neither do I, sir," he admitted, desperate. "But we don't have another option. If we don't act now, this could end in tragedy… This is the only chance we have!"

"Give me five minutes in there, sir," Jim pleaded. "If I can't do anything, go ahead with your plan."

The chief let out a deep breath, visibly torn.

Finally, he gave a cautious nod.

"You have three minutes. Not a second more."

Then, raising his voice, he turned his attention to the tour bus still parked nearby, with the terrified tourists inside.

"Someone get that bus out of here! Move these people—they're in danger!"

The driver, who was still behind the wheel, received the order from an officer and quickly started the engine. He was instructed to take the passengers back to their hotel until further notice.

One of the officers approached Jim and Dimitri, handing them bulletproof vests. Dimitri put his on immediately, while Jim, with a determined expression, removed his gun and handed it over. Dimitri took it with obvious concern.

"You better come out of there in one piece, buddy."

Jim gave a tense smile and murmured as he adjusted his vest,

"That's the plan."

Taking one last breath, Jim stepped toward the laundromat, raising his hands in a gesture of peace. This was the moment—to change the course of the situation... or sink with it.

He clenched his jaw, feeling frustration burn inside him. Through the glass, he could see Jack clinging to Lori, the gun still pressed firmly against her temple.

From a near distance, Dimitri quickly assessed the scene and murmured,

"We can't force the door open without putting her in danger. We have to get him to open it himself."

Jim nodded and took a deep breath. His voice had to make the difference. He moved as close as possible to the locked door and, with all the calm he could muster, spoke:

"Jack, I'm Jim. Listen to me, please. Let me come in, and we'll talk... just you and me. No one wants to hurt you. Tell me what you need."

Jack whipped his head around, his wild-eyed stare filled with sheer panic.

"I can't trust anyone! They'll take me down the moment I let her go!" he shouted, his voice cracking with desperation.

Jim shook his head, his tone firm but conciliatory.

"No one's going to take you down if you cooperate. Just talk to me. Tell me what you need. Open the door... please."

Jack was breathing heavily. For a moment, he seemed to hesitate.

But then, a loud noise from the alley behind the building shattered the tension like a gunshot in the night.

Jack flinched, his instincts kicking in, and he tightened his grip on Lori. She let out a sharp gasp of pain.

"No! They won't take me down!" Jack shouted; his eyes wild. With a sudden, jerky movement, he started backing toward the back room.

Panic surged up Jim's throat.

Dimitri cursed under his breath, casting a sharp glance at the sniper on the rooftop.

Jack dragged Lori further into the laundromat, away from the storefront.

Jim couldn't allow it. He had to act now.

The tension was thick enough to cut with a knife. Jim was just about to spring into action when the rooftop sniper, following the police chief's orders, aimed precisely at Jack's head. But Jack kept moving, using Lori as a human shield.

"Sir, I don't have a clear shot…" the sniper reported through his earpiece.

The police chief, his brow furrowed and jaw clenched, didn't hesitate.

"Fire as soon as you have a clear shot!"

"No!" Jim shouted.

For a split second, Jack was exposed… and then, a muffled gunshot shattered the silence.

At that precise moment, Jack shifted just a few inches to the left.

The bullet shattered the glass door into a thousand pieces, grazing his ear before embedding itself in the metal of one of the dryers.

The sniper's shot had missed by a mere fraction of a second.

Jim's head pounded in his chest as he saw Jack tremble, his eyes now filled with both panic and fury. His life had just been directly threatened, and now, more than ever, he was on the verge of a reckless reaction.

Without thinking, Jim stepped through the destroyed door, carefully manoeuvring around the shards of glass on the floor. He had no other choice. The situation was more dangerous than ever, but he had to disarm Jack.

"Jim, no!" Dimitri shouted.

But Jim wasn't listening to anyone anymore—only to his instincts.

With his hands raised and all the intensity he could muster, he exclaimed:

"Jack, it doesn't have to end like this!"

The police chief shouted orders to the officers, who cautiously moved closer, ready to tighten the perimeter and block any possible escape.

Meanwhile, Dimitri, fearing for his reckless partner, positioned himself near the shattered door. From there, he had a clear view of everything, ready to intervene the moment he got a signal.

On the rooftop, the sniper waited for new orders, but now Jim was in the line of fire, making any shot nearly impossible.

Lori, still trapped in Jack's grip, couldn't take her eyes off Jim. Their gaze met amid the chaos, and for a fleeting moment, relief crossed her face. She didn't feel alone in this nightmare anymore. But at the same time, fear for Jim was evident in her eyes.

Then Jim noticed that Jack was swaying, on the verge of collapse. He was nervous, exhausted, as if the weight of the situation was crushing him.

Only then did Jim realize the dark stain spreading beneath Jack's hood—the bullet had grazed him, tearing through his ski mask and slicing the skin above his ear. Blood trickled down slowly, sliding down his neck and soaking his jacket.

Jim seized the moment.

"Jack! Listen to me!" he urged, his voice firm but almost desperate. "You're running out of options!"

Jack's gaze was distant, but he still refused to let go of Lori.

Jim took advantage of that momentarily distraction and tried to move closer, but Jack reacted instantly, tightening his grip on Lori.

"No! Don't take another step... or I'll kill her!" he shouted, his voice breaking, his eyes glossy with emotion.

Jim saw it clearly: Jack didn't want to kill anyone.

"Jack... let her go... please," Jim said calmly, choosing his words with care. "If you need a hostage, take me instead... They'll listen to you."

Jack was breathing heavily, his eyes filled with anguish.

"I know you don't want to do this," Jim continued, his tone firm yet understanding. "Put the gun down. We can still fix this."

Outside, the tension was unbearable. The officers kept their weapons raised, ready to fire at the slightest sign of danger.

The police chief checked his watch, his brow furrowed. He had given Jim three minutes. Ten had passed—long, intense, nerve-wrecking minutes.

"Prepare the assault team," he ordered tensely.

"No!" Dimitri intervened, stepping forward. "Give him some more time—he's negotiating with him."

Inside the laundromat, the situation grew more fragile by the second.

Jack tightened his grip on Lori, his desperation evident in every tense muscle of his body. Suddenly, he turned the gun and aimed it directly at Jim.

Lori held her breath.

"No... Jim..." she whispered, terrified.

Jim forced himself to stay calm, his gaze locked onto Jack's, his voice unwavering.

"Jack, tell me what happened. I promise I'll speak on your behalf. If you lower the gun now, you'll only face a charge for assault. But if you kill someone... there will be nothing I can do for you. That means life in prison."

Jack swallowed hard; his pulse unsteady. "You have a choice to make," Jim added.

"We can sit down and talk. Like two people… Like two friends."

On the rooftop, the sniper had Jack in his sight, but Jim stood strategically in the way, blocking the shot.

"Listen to me, Jack," Jim continued, stepping forward again. "Outside, there's a sniper waiting for the order to take your down. But as long as we keep talking, I'll stay right here, in the line of fire, to stop them. They'll have to shoot me first."

Jack closed his eyes for a second, his breathing uneven and erratic. He was distracted.

When he opened them again, something in his expression had changed.

And then, with a shaky sigh, he loosened his grip on Lori.

She didn't hesitate for even a second. In a swift movement, she ran toward Jim, taking refuge beside him.

"Are you okay?" Jim asked, his gaze filled with concern.

Lori nodded slightly.

Jim turned his gaze to Jack.

"Jack, she's going to walk out that door. Let her go. I promised I would stay, and I will. We'll talk."

Before Jack could respond, Lori took a deep breath and stepped forward.

"No," she said firmly. "I'm staying too."

Jim looked at her in surprise.

"Lori… I need you to leave. I need you to warn the people outside that I'm going to get him to come out peacefully. Tell them not to shoot, not to intervene."

"No, Jim," she replied with determination. "I'm not leaving you alone. Besides, there's strength in numbers. If there are two of us defending him, they won't dare shoot us." She added with a mischievous smile.

Jack blinked, unsure of how to react. He seemed truly confused. He held the gun firmly, pointing it at both of them, his stare empty yet filled with desperation. His glassy eyes reflected the internal storm consuming him, as if he were on the verge of breaking down in tears.

Finally, he removed his ski mask and spoke. His voice came out shaky, as if each word took more effort than the last.

"I… I was loyal, efficient, and punctual. I worked at the same company for thirty years…" he murmured, his voice cracking.

He paused, swallowing hard.

"They changed owners, computerizing every-thing… reduced staff and fired everyone who was no longer needed…"

Each sentence seemed to choke him, suffocated by anguish, as a lump in his throat threatened to consume him.

As he spoke, his grip on the gun loosened slightly.

Jim, watching him with growing concern, seized the moment to take another step closer. But the instant he moved, Jack reacted immediately, raising the gun again and aiming it firmly at him.

Lori remained steadfast beside Jim, refusing to move away, despite his attempts to shield her by positioning himself in front of her.

The air in the room grew even heavier, thick with suffocating tension.

"No, I know you don't believe me…"—his eyes filled with tears, but anger in his voice remained evident.

Jim, never breaking eye contact with Jack, remained calm, his voice soft yet firm.

"Jack… I do believe you. Unfortunately, this happens every day… but it's not the end of the world. You'll find another job."

Jack repeated the words in a murmur, as if testing them in his own mouth.

"Another job…"

His shoulders slumped, and his voice dropped to a whisper, as if speaking to himself.

"I was a section chief at the assembly plant of a well-known car brand…"

His gaze drifted into the distance, lost in memories, watching his life crumble before his eyes.

Lori, who had remained silent until now, stepped forward cautiously. Her expression was gentle, filled with understanding.

Jim tried to stop her, slightly positioning himself in front of her, but Lori stood firm.

"They haven't been fair to you, Jack," she said, her voice full of sorrow. "But you can still find another job. You're young, you have options."

Jack let out a bitter laugh, a dry chuckle that echoed cruelly through the room.

"Young?" he repeated in disbelief. "At forty-eight, no one wants you for a job anymore!"

Despite his deep sadness and desperation, Jack didn't look his age. He had a surprisingly youthful appearance, as if his exterior was trying to deny the weight of his reality.

His frustration and despair hung heavy in the air.

"Besides, I don't know how to do anything else. My whole life, I worked on the car assembly line. And now... now that doesn't exist anymore."

His voice broke, and for a moment, he wasn't an armed and dangerous man—he was just someone who had lost everything: his job, his identity, his purpose.

He lowered his gaze, defeated, and whispered:

"For me, it is the end of the world."

With that, Jack stopped pointing the gun at them and raised the barrel to his own temple.

"No, Jack! Don't do anything reckless!" Jim shouted, lunging toward him.

Jack immediately stepped back two paces, his gaze unfocused, his hand trembling.

"Don't come any closer... please... let me go with dignity," he pleaded, his voice broken.

"No, Jack. That's not dignity—that's cowardice," Jim replied, his voice firm and resolute as he took a step forward. His eyes were filled with determination.

"Do you really want your family to think you're a coward? Don't do it, Jack!" he added forcefully, reaching out to him, offering a way out.

"Give me the gun... my friend," Jim whispered, his hand still extended.

Jack stared at him, his face etched with pain and bitterness.

"What family?" he responded with resentment, as if those words hurt him more that Jim could have imagined.

Lori, who had been silently observing, stepped forward, her gaze filled with sorrow and empathy. She knew that words of comfort might be useless at this moment, but she still felt the need to try—to make him see that there was something beyond his pain.

"You don't have a wife? Children, Jack?" she asked gently, her voice trembling with understanding, as she moved cautiously, making sure her tone was not confrontational but a sincere attempt to connect.

Jack tensed immediately. His face twisted as if a sharp pain had pierced him, his eyes flashing with a mix of anger and sorrow, drowning in desperation.

"My wife left me…" he murmured, his voice shattered. "She took my son when I lost my job and was left with nothing… She abandoned me with nothing."

His breathing was ragged, each word hitting his chest like a blow.

Lori watched him with compassion.

"Jack, forgive me for saying this, but that was cruel of her," she said sincerely. "Maybe she didn't love you enough. That's not love."

She paused, searching his eyes.

"You can still rebuild your life. Jack, everything has a solution... except death."

Jack clenched his jaw, his gaze lost in the void.

Jim, seeing the weight of those words pressing down on him, took a deep breath. When he spoke, his voice was firm but gentle, trying to reach the man still buried beneath the anguish.

"Jack, they let you fall, but that doesn't mean you have to keep falling. You can still get back up. There are ways to rebuild your life."

He paused, giving Jack a moment to process it, before calmly adding:

"But for that, you have to make a decision. Are going to keep losing everything... or are you going to fight for something better?"

Jack slowly lowered the gun and looked at both of them, his face a mix of confusion, pain, and frustration. But for the first time in a long while, he seemed to be listening.

Jim stepped forward with steady steps, slow but firm. Gently, he slid the gun from Jack's hands. Jack did not resist.

"Jack," Jim said firmly, "I will help you find a new job. That's a promise. When you serve your sentence—which will be short—I'll help you reintegrate into society."

"And so will I!" Lori exclaimed with a determined smile.

Jim looked at her in surprise before returning the smile. It was over.

Cautiously, he and Lori positioned themselves in front of Jack to shield him as they moved toward the exit, stepping over the shattered glass at the entrance.

"We're coming out! Don't shoot!" Jim shouted, raising his hand in a stopping gesture.

They emerged through the doorway with Jack behind them, his hands raised, walking unsteadily. His face reflected fear, but also a glimmer of hope.

The air was tense, each second dragging along an invisible danger. Jim and Lori moved forward, keeping Jack protected behind them. Everything seemed under control.

Until…

A shot tore through the silence. A sharp, brutal crack.

Jim felt the hot rush of air as the bullet almost grazed his cheek.

The bullet struck Jack square in the forehead… and in an instant, he collapsed to the ground.

"Noooo!" Jim's scream ripped through the air—raw, helpless.

Lori stood frozen; her eyes locked on Jack's lifeless body. The bullet lodged perfectly in the centre of his forehead, a thin trickle of blood the only movement left in him…

Jim remained still, his mind refusing to accept what his eyes were seeing. After everything he had done to save him… one single shot had destroyed it all.

Lori stepped closer to Jim, her face pale, her eyes filled with tears. There were no words. Only the crushing silence of the inevitable.

Jim turned to Dimitri, his expression a storm of disbelief and contained fury. He couldn't believe what had just happened. Every effort, every word, every attempt at persuasion… ruined in a single instant.

Dimitri, his lips pressed tightly, his jaw clenched, shook his head. His eyes mirrored helplessness. He hadn't been able to stop it either.

A wave of indignation surged through Jim's body. He spun toward the police chief, his voice burning with rage.

"Why did you do it?! He was surrendering!"

The police chief met his gaze with a severe expression, devoid of remorse.

"I gave a direct order," he responded coldly. "As soon as the assailant stepped outside and was within range… shoot."

Jim clenched his fists, feeling a knot tighten in his stomach. He looked down at Jack's lifeless body on the ground, the blood barely seeping out. It didn't have to end this way.

Lori covered her mouth, stifling a sob. Her eyes shimmered with tears of both fury and sorrow.

"We had convinced him…" she whispered. "He was willing to surrender!"

Jim took a deep breath, trying to steady himself, but his chest burned with frustration. He glanced at the officers surrounding the scene, some still gripping their weapons.

"It wasn't necessary," he finally said, his voice breaking. "He wasn't a murderer. Just a desperate man."

But it didn't matter anymore. Jack was dead. And no apology, no justification, would change that fact.

While they remained at the scene, ambulances arrived swiftly, prepared to treat any injuries— though, fortunately, there were no other victims.

Paramedics moved efficiently, checking if anyone needed assistance. The forensic team would begin their work later, once it was time to remove Jack's body.

Jim turned to Lori, whose face still bore the traces of anguish, her eyes still wet with fresh tears.

The weight of everything that had happened seemed to settle heavily on him.

"I'm sorry," he said, his voice thick with guilt. The words felt like a confession, as if, somehow, he had failed. He hesitated before asking softly, "Are you okay?"

Lori nodded slowly, though the pain was still visible in her eyes. It was over now—or at least, it seemed that way.

The afternoon was beginning to fade, and the entire day had been marked by this agonizing ordeal.

"Do you need a ride home? Or anywhere you'd like," Dimitri offered kindly, aware of all she had endured.

Lori considered it for a moment before shaking her head gently.

"Thank you, but that won't be necessary. I need to stop by the travel agency to file my report for the day, and it's nearby," she replied, grateful but visibly exhausted.

Jim gave a small, sombre smile and nodded. "Yeah, I need to file a report too. I hope I see you around… but under better circumstances," he added, his tone lightening slightly, though the sadness never fully left his face.

Lori met his gaze, her eyes filled with a mixture of gratitude and sorrow.

"Yes, I'd like that," she replied softly, her voice laden with emotion. "Thank you, Jim. Dimitri…" she said in farewell before turning to leave, each step taking her farther away—but with the lingering feeling that this tragedy would weigh on them all for a long time to come.

ROMANCE AT HAND

ONE SEEMINGLY ORDINARY evening, after finishing their shift, Jim and Dimitri decided to stop by a pub for a few beers before heading home. True to his considerate nature, Dimitri calls his wife to let her know he'll be home a little later, reassuring her that everything is fine. While on the phone, he thinks about picking up some sweets and flowers for her and the kids—a small surprise, just because. That is Dimitri in a nutshell—affectionate, thoughtful, and unwaveringly devoted to his family.

As they settle in, enjoying the relaxed atmosphere, their conversation drifts toward an amusing topic: the upcoming wedding of a fellow officer, to which they are both invited. Between sips of beer and easy laughter, they debate what to wear, what gift would be appropriate, and even try to guess what will be on the menu.

Seated at the bar near a large window overlooking the street, Dimitri's sharp eyes catch a familiar figure passing by.

"Isn't that Lori?" he asks, leaning slightly toward the glass.

Jim follows his gaze, his expression shifting from curiosity to recognition in an instant.

"Yeah!" He sets down his beer and stands abruptly, driven by instinct.

Without a second thought, he strides toward the door, pushes it open, and calls out:

"Lori!"

She stops mid-step and turns, momentarily surprised. But as soon as she recognizes him, a genuine smile lights up her face.

"Hey!" she greets, her voice bright despite the long day.

Noticing the hour, Jim tilts his head. "Just finished your shift?"

"Yeah, finally," she sighs, stretching her shoulders. "Guiding a group of tireless tourists is no joke. But tomorrow's another day."

"You're telling me," Jim chuckles. "We just wrapped up too—grabbing a beer before heading home."

A brief pause. Then, with an easy grin, he adds, "Hey, why don't you join us? First round's on me."

Lori hesitates for a split second, but the warmth in his smile makes the decision for her.

"Alright, sounds good," Lori agrees with a bright smile. "Thanks!"

Jim holds the door open as she steps inside, while Dimitri watches them with an amused, knowing grin.

The moment she reaches the bar, Dimitri stands, greeting her with his usual enthusiasm.

"Hey! How's it going? What'll you have?" he asks with an easy-going grin.

"A beer would be great, thanks," Lori replies, sliding onto the stool next to Jim.

The conversation flows effortlessly, punctuated by laughter and lively exchanges. Dimitri, ever the storyteller, entertains them with a few amusing anecdotes, earning hearty laughs from his companions. The pub's warm, relaxed atmosphere makes it easy to unwind, and time slips by unnoticed.

Eventually, Dimitri checks his watch and exhales dramatically.

"Well, folks, I'd better call it a night... If I stay any longer, my wife might be waiting with the rolling pin in hand," he jokes with a wink.

Jim and Lori chuckle, shaking their heads. Before leaving, Dimitri gestures to the bartender.

"Go on, have another round on me. It's been a pleasure, Lori," he says warmly before turning to Jim. "See you tomorrow."

"See you tomorrow, Dimitri!" Jim replies, lifting his beer in a casual toast.

"The pleasure was mine. Good night… and thanks for the drink!" Lori adds with a grateful smile.

"No problem. Enjoy! See your around," Dimitri says, raising a hand in farewell as he heads for the door.

As they watch him leave, Jim and Lori exchange a glance—one of those unspoken moments of understanding—and almost simultaneously break into a knowing smile. With a relaxed gesture, Jim signals the bartender for another round, courtesy of Dimitri.

The night stretches on at its own unhurried pace, the conversation meandering easily between stories and laughter. At one point, a brief lull settles between them, only for both to start speaking at the exact same time. Their words overlap in a jumble, sparking an amused silence.

They pause, exchange a look, and burst into laughter.

"You first," Jim says with a grin, motioning for her to go ahead.

"Thanks. I was just about to say that your partner is really nice and funny," Lori remarks with a warm smile.

Jim nods, feeling a genuine sense of pride for his friend.

"You have no idea," he replies fondly. Seizing the moment, he begins to share how he first met Dimitri and how their relationship evolved—from instructor and trainee to colleagues and, eventually, close friends. He talks about Dimitri's large family, his unwavering devotion as a husband and father, and his ever-present sense of humour—a quality that, according to Jim, makes even the longest patrol shift more enjoyable.

As he recounts some of Dimitri's stories, someone nearby spills a beer. Almost instinctively, Jim is reminded of that first day... the collision, the spilled coffee... A smile tugs at his lips, and without thinking too much, he remarks with a playful grin:

"Speaking of stains... you still haven't sent me the dry-cleaning bill for your blouse!"

Lori laughs, waving him off.

"Oh, come on! It's nothing," she says with a teasing roll of her eyes.

"I'm serious," Jim insists. "Send me the bill—I always keep my promises."

She shakes her head, still smiling.

"Thanks, but that's ancient history. Forget it, Jim," she says with an amused disbelief. "You're sweet for offering, but it never even crossed my mind. These things can happen to anyone!"

Jim studies her for a moment, as if weighing something. Then, with a decisive smile, he says, "Well, in that case… I'll have to take you to dinner to make up for it."

Lori lets out a light laugh, but then pauses, thoughtful. After a beat, she grins.

"Alright, I accept! That, I'd actually like!"

"Whenever you're free. How about this Saturday!" he suggests, his excitement evident.

Lori pulls a regretful face.

"Ugh… I've got a lot of tourist groups right now, and I'll be swamped. Sorry," she says sincerely. "But maybe next week. I'll let you know."

Jim nods with an understanding smile.

"Deal. I'll be waiting for your message."

With that, he takes a card from his wallet and hands it to her.

Lori accepts it with a smile—then, without hesitation, pulls out one of her own.

"Thanks. Here's mine… Feel free to call me anytime," Lori said with a playful wink.

She flashed him a quick smile before returning to the conversation, but Jim already knew—sooner or later, that dinner would happen.

After exchanging a few more anecdotes, Jim's tone grew more serious as he brought up the day of the incident when Jack took her hostage. He recalled how Lori had shown remarkable courage amidst the chaos, stepping in with a level of empathy that had truly stood out. He admitted that he'd been impressed by the way she spoke to Jack, managing to reach him when few others could.

"You have a real gift with people, Lori," he said with conviction.

She looked visibly flattered. "Thank you," she replied sincerely. "Honestly, I love working with people—that's why I'm a tour guide." She gestured lightly, as if the connection were obvious. "It's the closest thing to being an 'air hostess,' which is my real dream. For now, this is a stepping stone while I work toward making it happen. And honestly? I'm loving it."

Her enthusiasm was infectious, and Jim found himself smiling.

"Really? You want to be an 'air hostess'?" he asked, intrigued.

"Well, nowadays, they call them 'flight attendants' or 'cabin crew,'" she corrected with a soft laugh, her eyes alight with excitement. "But yeah—I've already submitted my CV and all the necessary paperwork. Just waiting to hear back."

Jim nodded approvingly; his smile warm.

"I think you'd make an incredible… flight attendant," he said, playfully adjusting his wording. "And a stunning one, too. Wishing you all the best."

She let out a light laugh, acknowledging the compliment with a knowing glance.

"Thanks, that's very sweet of you."

"Which airline?" he asked curiously.

"Hawaiian Airlines," she answered, her smile bright and hopeful.

Jim's brows lifted slightly, impressed.

"That sounds amazing. I have no doubt I'll see you soaring through the skies soon."

She held his gaze for a moment, feeling an unexpected warmth at his encouragement.

"Let's hope you're right."

"I'm sure of it," Jim assured her. Then, with a mischievous grin, he added, "Besides… you'd have the perfect excuse to fly to Hawaii whenever you wanted!"

"My parents actually live there—in Hawaii," Lori said enthusiastically.

Jim's eyebrows lifted in surprise. "Really? That's great."

A brief pause settled between them before Lori, her expression turning mischievous, added,

"I'm Hawaiian."

Jim narrowed his eyes at her, a playful smile tugging at his lips.

"Are you now?" he said, studying her with exaggerated curiosity. "I wouldn't have guessed...

Those blue eyes—or are they grey?" He tilted his head, pretending to scrutinize her. "And that honey-coloured hair..."

Lori let out a bright laugh.

"My dad is full Hawaiian, but my mom is from Utah. Blonde, blue-eyed..." she explained, shaking her head fondly.

"Ah, I see," Jim mused, nodding sagely. "And I'm from London, then!—son of an Irish father and a Londoner mother..."

Lori smirked. "Really? I never would've guessed—you don't exactly give off that stiff, afternoon-tea-and-crumpets vibe."

Jim straightened his posture, adopting an air of exaggerated refinement. "I prefer tea and scones, my dear," he declared in his best posh English accent, utterly determined to make her laugh.

Their laughter came easily, the conversation flowing effortlessly between them as if they'd known each other for years.

For a moment, Jim considered inviting Lori to his fellow officer's wedding—a perfect opportunity to spend more time together. But he hesitated. They had only just met, and he didn't want to rush things or make her feel uncomfortable. Maybe another time.

Before they realized it, the evening had slipped away.

"Wow!" Jim exclaimed, checking the time. "That flew by. I've been so caught up talking with you that I didn't even notice... But I don't know about you—I have an early morning tomorrow."

Lori's eyes widened in surprise before she let out a sigh.

"Oh, same! I must be up at seven to meet my early-bird tour group. At exactly eight, we're heading to the Statue of Liberty." She let out a playful groan. "It's going to be a long day."

"That sounds like an interesting job," Jim commented with a smile.

"It is—I love it. But sometimes it can be exhausting," Lori admitted with a small laugh.

Jim nodded in understanding, then stood up. "Then we'd better call it a night," he said.

"Want a ride home? My car's just around the corner."

Lori hesitated for a moment before nodding with a grateful smile.

"Alright, thanks. If it's not too much trouble…"

"Not at all!" Jim assured her.

As they drove in his car, their conversation continued effortlessly, sprinkled with laughter and shared stories. When they finally arrived at Lori's building, they paused at the entrance, exchanging an easy smile.

"Well… thanks. Bye," Lori said, taking a small step toward the door.

Jim watched her for a second before adding, "If you ever feel like grabbing a drink or just chatting, don't hesitate to call me. See you soon."

She gave him one last smile before heading inside.

As Jim drove away, he found himself still smiling. Maybe tonight had been more than just a pleasant conversation. Maybe it was the start of something more.

From that day on, Jim stopped pretending to be indifferent. He no longer hid the way his gaze instinctively wandered through the streets, scanning groups of tourists or buses bearing the log of Lori's agency. Whenever he had the chance, he stole a glance—hoping, just for a moment, to catch a glimpse of her, even from the distance.

It didn't take long for Dimitri to notice the shift in his friend, and he wasted no time teasing him about it.

"Jim, if I were twenty years younger, I'd give you some real competition for Lori," he said with a mischievous grin, nudging Jim with his elbow.

Jim rolled his eyes but couldn't suppress a smile. "Good thing for me you're very happily married."

Dimitri let out a hearty laugh, nodding proudly. "You can say that again! I wouldn't trade my Athina for anything in the world. She's, my soulmate."

Jim smiled, watching the way Dimitri spoke about his wife—with absolute certainty, with love so solid and unwavering that there wasn't a trace of doubt in his voice.

And for the first time in a long while, Jim found himself wondering if he might one day find something like that.

If, perhaps, Lori could be the beginning of that answer.

The thought settled in his chest, warm and undeniably pleasing.

The days passed, and soon, Jim and Dimitri found themselves at their fellow officer's wedding—a lively celebration filled with laughter, stories, and the kind of memories that only good friends could create.

Since that last beer together, Jim and Lori hadn't managed to meet up again. Their encounters had been quite fleeting—an occasional passing on the street, a quick glance from afar, or a hurried greeting as she guided a group of tourists from one landmark to another. She was always busy, fully immersed in her work, and though her smiles were genuine, time was never on their side. Still, each brief exchange left Jim with the undeniable feeling that their story wasn't over.

Every now and then, fate seemed to push them together at a coffee shop—mornings spent waiting for their to-go cups before starting the day or during a quick afternoon break. In these small, stolen moments, they greeted each other with knowing smiles and, almost as a ritual, exchanged comments about their mutual love for coffee. To both of them, it wasn't just a habit—it was a necessary indulgence, a quiet moment of comfort in the middle of their chaotic schedules. No matter the hour or how exhausted they were, a steaming cup of coffee was always a welcome sight.

One afternoon, determined to break the cycle of chance meetings, Jim sent her a message.

"I still owe you that dinner. When are you free?"

He didn't have to wait long for a response. Lori replied almost immediately, letting him know she was free that Saturday evening and Sunday morning.

Without hesitation, they made plans for dinner on Saturday night. Nothing too formal—just something casual and friendly.

Or at least, that was the initial idea.

The evening turned out even better than expected. The atmosphere was effortlessly inviting—starting with beers and leading into a light dinner at a charming pub, one of those cozy spots with dim lighting, soft background music, and just the right touch of warmth. It wasn't a formal venue, but in its own way, it carried a quiet intimacy—one that felt distinctly romantic.

Both of them had chosen looks that were casual yet refined. Jim wore dark jeans with a crisp blue shirt—his favourite colour—topped with a blazer, his black loafers completing the effortlessly polished look. Lori, on the other hand, went for black jeans that flattered her figure, a soft pink blouse that added a fresh, feminine touch, and a black leather jacket that gave her an effortlessly stylish edge. To complete the look, she wore classic black heels that elevated her ensemble just enough.

As the night unfolded, so did their conversation, deepening with each shared story.

Lori told Jim about her childhood in Maui, where she and her sister had grown up surrounded by breathtaking landscapes and a strong sense of community. She spoke about her parents—their whirlwind romance that had started in a Hawaiian hospital, where her mother, a nurse form Utah, was working at the time and met her father, a patient undergoing treatment. Their love had been fast but undeniable, leading to a marriage that stood the test of time.

Jim listened intently, drawn in by the warmth in her voice as she spoke about her family.

Between stories and laughter, the evening flowed effortlessly. At one point, they decided to play a round of darts, a spontaneous choice that quickly turned competitive.

Lori won—just barely—grinning in satisfaction while Jim shook his head in mock indignation.

"You cheated," he accused, crossing his arms. "You stepped over the throwing line."

Lori let out a bright laugh, tilting her head playfully. "Oh, come on! A sore loser already?"

Jim smirked, pretending to consider her words. "Not a sore loser—just a man in search of justice."

She chuckled, shaking her head.

It had, without a doubt, been a great date.

One day, Jim's middle sister, Nicky—a military paramedic—returned home on special leave. One of her teammates from ECHO-6, an elite six-person unit, was getting married, and she had the privilege of inviting whoever she wanted from the family.

The wedding was for the squad's sergeant, Sergeant Corelli—a man of Italian descent—who was now marrying Francesca, a lively and charming Italian woman. Jim didn't know him well, but he vaguely remembered meeting him once at a party where they had both been invited. Though their conversation had been brief, Jim had come away with the impression of a serious professional with a great sense of humour outside of work.

Without hesitation, Nicky handed an invitation to Jim and another to their younger brother, Andy. She knew the wedding would be a grand celebration, and the O'Hara siblings never missed an opportunity to enjoy moments like that together.

Jim accepted without a second thought, looking forward to the event. But almost immediately, his mind drifted to Lori. This time, he genuinely wanted to invite her—if she didn't already have plans. It was the perfect chance to spend time together, dance, and get to know each other better. Maybe even introduce her to Nicky and Andy.

However, as the days passed, the right moment to ask her never seemed to come. Lori was always busy, effortlessly moving from one place to another, guiding tourists with that boundless energy that defined her. Jim didn't want to extend the invitation in passing, rushed between her tours, nor did he want to resort to a simple WhatsApp message—it felt too impersonal. He wanted to ask her properly, maybe over a coffee, in a quiet moment where he could see her reaction.

But time worked against him, and the opportunity slipped through his fingers.

Before he knew it, the wedding day had arrived. As Jim got ready to attend, a slight sense of regret lingered. He hadn't been able to invite Lori—not even at the last minute—because he refused to do it in a way that felt distant or thoughtless. Despite his best efforts, the days had simply gone by too quickly.

Even so, he wasn't discouraged. He was convinced that another chance would come. Weddings were a common occurrence in his life, and who knew? Maybe next time, the circumstances would be different—maybe fate would finally be on his side.

Perhaps this just wasn't the right moment. But when it was, he had no doubt he'd recognize it.

As he adjusted the knot of his tie in front of the mirror, Jim smiled with quiet determination. Next time, he wouldn't let the opportunity slip away. If necessary, he'd stop traffic just to ask her.

The three O'Hara siblings gathered, as they always did, to attend the wedding together— keeping their long-standing tradition of showing up as an inseparable team. Upon arriving at the venue, they were introduced to Nicky's team: Colonel Williams, Major Taylor, Captain Campbell, and the newest member of the unit—a young soldier about the same age as Andy, the youngest O'Hara sibling.

And off course, Nicky was there too, alongside the groom, Sergeant Corelli. With everyone present, ECHO-6 was complete. They weren't just a squad—they were like family.

The wedding, though military in style, struck the perfect balance between elegance and simplicity. The groom and his groomsmen wore Marine Corps uniforms, but without the full ceremonial formality, giving the event a refined yet relaxed atmosphere.

Colonel Williams had the honour of being the best man, while Major Taylor and Captain Campbell stood by Corelli's side as groomsmen. On the bride's side, Francesca's younger sister, Emily, served as maid of honour, accompanied by Georgina—the colonel's sister-in-law—and a third bridesmaid, a military woman closely tied to ECHO-6, though not officially part of the team.

However, an unexpected delay prevented that last bridesmaid from arriving on time, and in her place, her twin sister stepped in at the last minute. Though not an official member of the unit, her connection through her sister made her a familiar presence.

Her sudden appearance caught many by surprise—but no one was more stunned than Jim.

It wasn't just that he hadn't expected to see her in this wedding. It was how breathtaking she looked.

That last-minute bridesmaid was none other than… Lori.

At that precise moment, Jim couldn't shake the feeling that this wasn't just a coincidence—it had to be fate working its magic.

But Jim wasn't the only one caught off guard. Lori, too, was surprised to see him there, at the same wedding, as if destiny had orchestrated their meeting. Was this really just a random twist of fate, or was there something more behind their unexpected reunion?

That day turned out to be far more significant than either of them had imagined. Neither had expected to cross paths like this—at the same wedding, as if something greater had brought them together.

The ceremony was beautiful, filled with emotional, heartfelt moments. Later, during the reception, tradition kept the wedding party—bridesmaids, groomsmen, and best man—by the couple's side, meaning Jim and Lori were seated at separate tables.

Despite the distance, they couldn't help but glance at each other throughout the evening, as if an invisible thread bound them together.

When the time came for the dance, Jim didn't hesitate to ask Lori to join him on the dance floor. Though Lori had a few dance commitments lined up, they managed to spend the rest of the evening together, enjoying each other's company.

Meanwhile, Lori's twin sister, Lily, arrived late due to a mission abroad. Her leave had been delayed by several hours, so she walked in just as the celebration was getting underway. Jim, seeing her for the first time, almost mistook her for Lori. They looked so alike that, had it not been for the army uniform Lily was wearing, it would have been impossible to tell them apart.

Of course, Lori wasted no time in introducing her sister, and Jim, delighted by the coincidence, invited her to dance as well. He couldn't help but marvel at how identical the two were. Lori and Lily were like two peas in a pod! However, despite their striking resemblance, Lily, being the older of the two by nine minutes, had a slightly distinct personality.

Both sisters shared a genuine passion for human interaction. However, Lily was bold and daring, unafraid of blood or risky situations, which made her stand out in her role as a military nurse. Lori, on the other hand, tended to avoid such intense scenarios, although she has her own form of bravery—one that she rarely gives herself credit for. Her charisma and natural ability to connect with people make her excel as a tour guide, a job she loved, even if she saw it as only a stepping stone. Her true dream was to soar through the skies, and with her remarkable people skills, she hoped to one day become a flight attendant.

Throughout their lives, very few people could tell them apart at first glance—except for their parents, of course. The confusion amused the sisters, though they weren't the type to play tricks on others by switching places. They reserved that for rare, light-hearted moments.

That night, filled with laughter, dancing, and the unexpected reunion, Jim couldn't shake the feeling that fate had orchestrated this meeting. And for the first time in a long time, he allowed himself to believe that maybe, just maybe, he was exactly where he was meant to be.

One of the members of the ECHO-6 team, Major Taylor, had met Lily, Lori's twin sister, years ago at a remote field hospital, where she had treated him for injuries. Since that day, he had been captivated by Lily, and now, at this wedding, they were reunited—this time, a reunion that would spark an even stronger connection between them. Could this, perhaps, be the start of another beautiful love story?

Continuing with the theme of love stories, Andy, Jim's younger brother, took a liking to the bride's maid of honour and younger sister, Emily. He asked her out to dance several times, and they quickly got on very well! Perhaps, yet another love story!

This wedding seemed to hold something truly special. Fate, once again, appeared to be weaving its magic. After all, fate always knows best… and it always wins!

Meanwhile, Jim and Lori spent much of the night on the dance floor, lost in the rhythm of the music, as if the world had shrunk to just the two of them. Both loved to dance, but Lori quickly noticed that Jim had an exceptional talent for every style, from the classic and romantic to the more modern beats. He moved with a confidence and elegance that left her pleasantly surprised.

"You dance incredibly well," she remarked, smiling in admiration.

Jim let out a soft laugh and, with a carefree shrug, replied, "At home, Mom always taught us that a gentleman should know how to court, have good manners… and, of course, know how to dance."

Lori raised an eyebrow, amused. "So, dancing talent runs in the O'Hara family?"

"Without exception," Jim confirmed, a mix of pride and humour in his voice. "Mom O'Hara, the most refined of us all, personally made sure none of us ever stepped out of rhythm."

Lori couldn't help but laugh. The image of an elegant and demanding matriarch teaching her family to move with grace was both charming and endearing. And as Jim glided effortlessly across the dance floor, she had no doubt that his mother had done an impeccable job.

Jim glanced at her, mesmerized by the natural way she moved, with such grace and ease.

"You're not too bad yourself," he said, smiling, delighted by how perfectly they complemented each other.

"I just go with the flow with you!" she exclaimed, spinning lightly. "Because I love to dance!"

That night, amid laughter, perfectly synchronized steps, and knowing glances, Lori realized that their dance was more than just a fleeting moment. It reflected Jim's very essence: a man with charisma, respect for traditions, and a charm that was simply irresistible.

At one point during the night, Jim and Lori decided to take a break and enjoy a glass of champagne. Between laughter and tender glances, Jim invited her to step out onto the hotel terrace where the wedding was being held.

"Would you like some fresh air?" he asked with a smile.

Lori, grateful for the chance to catch her breath, happily agreed. Between the warmth of the dance and the excitement of the night, she was craving a moment of peace and fresh air.

Outside, the night breeze was cool and refreshing, a perfect contrast to the warmth of the ballroom. They stood there for a while, enjoying the quiet, their conversation flowing easily between them. But as the minutes passed, Lori began to shiver slightly. She had left her shawl inside, though deep down, she knew that her shivering wasn't just from the cold. It was something else—Jim's closeness was stirring something within her, a feeling she couldn't quite define. Was it simply his company... or was it something more?

Jim quickly noticed her discomfort. Without a word, he slipped off his jacket and draped it over her shoulders, the fabric warming her instantly.

He then moved closer, his presence surrounding her like a shield.

"Better like this?" he asked, his smile disarming and genuine.

Lori nodded, feeling the heat of his gesture spread through her. The touch of his jacket, the proximity of his body—everything about the moment made her heart race.

"Yes… thank you, Jim." Her voice was soft, but in her mind, one question echoed: *Where did a man like this come from?* It all felt surreal, like she was dreaming.

But Jim didn't stop there. His gaze shifted, growing deeper, more intense. Then, in a whisper laced with sincerity, he said:

"Lori… I really like you."

Her heart skipped a beat, the words sending a wave of warmth through her. A soft blush coloured her cheeks as she met his gaze and, in a quiet voice, replied:

"I like you too, Jim."

Their eyes locked in the dim light of the terrace, and without a word, they moved closer, drawn together by an invisible force. Their lips met in a gentle, lingering kiss—soft, full of unspoken emotions. A kiss that, in the span of seconds, deepened and intensified, as if time itself had paused, allowing them to fully embrace the moment.

When they finally pulled away, they remained close, wrapped in a comfortable silence, gazing at the starry sky above them. Lori, still enveloped in Jim's jacket and the warmth of his embrace, felt a profound shift within her. This night wasn't just special—it felt like the beginning of something that could change everything.

At the wedding, Jim didn't miss the chance to introduce Lori to his siblings. From the moment they met, Nicky and Andy were immediately taken with her. Lori had a natural charisma, a warmth that seemed to seamlessly integrate into the O'Hara family dynamic, as if she had always been part of their circle. Her spontaneity, sense of humour, and effortless ability to engage in conversation made Nicky and Andy feel, within minutes, like they had known her forever.

That night, after the party, back at the family home, Nicky couldn't contain her excitement and approached Jim with a big grin.

"It's about time, big brother! At your age, you're about to miss the boat!" she teased with a playful laugh, giving him a light nudge on the arm. "I can't wait for your wedding."

Before Jim could respond, she added, eyes sparkling with enthusiasm, "Also... I want to be the maid of honour!"

From across the room, Andy, who had been listening in, jumped into the conversation with excitement.

"And I'll be your best man!" he shouted, his voice full of energy.

Jim snorted and shook his head, trying to hold back his amusement. "What are you two talking about? Relax, guys. Lori and I are still getting to know each other," he replied, a hint of incredulity in his tone.

But as the words left his mouth, a part of him knew they weren't entirely accurate. Yes, he and Lori still had a lot to learn about each other, but deep down, Jim was already certain of how he felt for her. It was more than just attraction—it was love. What he couldn't be sure of, however, was whether Lori felt the same way.

Nicky, crossing her arms with a mischievous glint in her eye, winked at him. "We're just practicing for the future."

"Very soon, I hope!" Andy added with a laugh.

Jim looked at them, pretending to be annoyed, but he couldn't hide the smile tugging at the corners of his lips. Though his siblings were teasing him, the idea of a future with Lori felt too good to dismiss outright.

Going along with the joke, Jim shifted his gaze to Nicky and, with a playful smirk, said, "Look who's talking. The one missing the boat is you. I'm a man, and that saying is usually for women." He laughed, thoroughly enjoying the banter.

Nicky rolled her eyes and crossed her arms, her expression mockingly indignant.

"Please. Me? Married? My Mr. Right only exists on the big screen… I'm holding out for Bond. James Bond," she said with a smirk, radiating confidence.

Jim raised an eyebrow, not buying it. "Right… except I couldn't help noticing the way you kept glancing at your captain. What's his name again? Oh yeah—Captain Campbell."

Nicky let out a laugh, but her cheeks betrayed her with the faintest blush.

"Oh, please! Don't be ridiculous. You know perfectly well that relationships within the team are strictly off-limits. And anyway… that guy's not exactly picky. If it has a chest, he's interested. He likes *everyone*. They don't call him Captain Casanova for nothing.

Jim smirked, leaning in with a teasing glint in his eye.

"Yeah, yeah… but out of all the gorgeous women at the wedding, guess who had his full attention? You."

"I'm the only one who hasn't fallen for his charm, and that bruises his ego. He's trying hard to reel me in, but I'm not falling for it," Nicky said with a shrug, pretending not to care. "I'm not going to be just another tick on his list."

Jim laughed out loud.

"Is that so? Because on the dance floor, you two looked pretty cozy. I mean, cheek to cheek? You weren't exactly keeping your distance."

"I was just playing along, letting him think he was getting somewhere," Nicky replied, trying to sound nonchalant—though her voice wavered just slightly.

Across the room, Andy started laughing— maybe a bit too loudly.

Jim turned to him, grinning. "And what about *you*, Casanova? Don't think we missed the way you were staring at that bridesmaid… What was her name—Emily?"

Andy held up his hands in surrender, eyes wide.

"Okay, okay—you caught me! I like her. She's sweet… and she's Italian! And those dimples? C'mon… *Mamma mia!*"

The laughter returned, and the three siblings continued joking well into the night, sharing anecdotes, laughter, and fond memories.

Eventually, fatigue started to set in, and one by one, they began to retire for the night. Jim, who would stay in the family apartment that night, bid them goodnight with a smile before heading to the guest bedroom, feeling more at home than ever.

The truth was, from that moment on, something in Jim and Lori's lives shifted—subtly, yet profoundly. Without needing words or formal agreements, they naturally gravitated toward each other, as if drawn by an invisible force.

In the bustle of the daily life, whether on the street or in the midst of work, their eyes instinctively sought one another. A fleeting glance across a crowded avenue, a moment when their gazes locked from a distance, was enough to bring a knowing smile to their lips. If the opportunity arose, they would exchange a discreet wave—small, almost imperceptible gestures, yet brimming with meaning.

Lori's tourists quickly picked up on these exchanges. More than one noticed how their tour guide greeted that handsome police officer with unmistakable enthusiasm. It wasn't just a casual, polite acknowledgment—there was a certain glow in her eyes whenever she saw him. Some travellers, keen observers of human nature, assumed they were a couple. Others, more romantic, were convinced they were already happily married. After all, there was something in the way Jim and Lori looked at each other—an unspoken connection, deeper than simple friendship.

As for Dimitri, he needed no assumptions. To him, everything was crystal clear. One look at his friend, and he knew the inevitable: Jim was in love, whether he admitted it or not. And more than that… he had found his soulmate.

Dimitri smiled to himself, almost smugly. There wasn't a doubt in his mind—sooner or later, there would be wedding bells. And, honestly, he couldn't be happier about it. Jim might not fully realize it yet, but Dimitri did. Fate had once again woven its magic.

With a teasing grin, he often quipped, "You'll invite me to your wedding, won't you? There's no way I'm missing that one!"

Jim would raise an eyebrow, feigning surprise, before breaking into laughter.

"Well, well, you too?" he'd say, shaking his head in amusement. "Why is everyone in such a hurry to see me married?"

Dimitri smirked. "Because it's about time you settle down. And let's be honest—you've got the perfect girl. What more do you need? Don't tell me you're still hesitating."

Jim sighed, his gaze drifting away. He knew Dimitri had a point. Every word rang true… yet a nagging doubt gnawed at him.

What if she didn't want the same things? What if, despite everything he felt, Lori didn't share his vision of the future?

Besides, they hadn't been together that long. Was he moving too fast? Was he diving headfirst into something too serious, too soon?

He exhaled slowly, steeling himself against his own uncertainties.

"I won't know until I ask her," he reminded himself. And when the time was right… he would.

THE PROPOSAL

AFTER THAT WEDDING that seemed written by fate, Jim tried not to come off as too eager, but he couldn't stop himself from texting Lori. He preferred messages to phone calls; afraid he might interrupt her work—or her life. His texts were simple, almost hesitant:

> *"How are you?"*
> *"Would you like to go out on Saturday? We could grab a drink, chat... or whatever you'd like. No pressure."*

He wanted to play it cool, but the truth was, he was aching to hear her voice, to see her again. Since that night, all they'd shared were stolen glances and rushed greetings in the middle of their busy routines. Not even that spontaneous, breath-stealing kiss at the wedding—which she'd seemed to enjoy just as much as he had—nor their mutual confession of attraction had quieted his desire to be near her.

He wanted more. He wanted to be with her—really be with her. To peel back the layers, to discover what lay behind her smile and those eyes that had completely captivated him. But most of all, he needed to know if she felt the same.

Jim wasn't the kind of man who lingered in limbo or wasted time on relationships with no direction. Usually, just a few dates were enough to tell if something had a future. But Lori… with her, everything felt different. There was a spark, something real. Her ease, her sincerity—everything about her made him think the feeling was mutual. And that only made him want her more.

So, slowly but surely, they started seeing each other more often. Each meeting flowed more easily, felt more natural, more needed. Until, almost without realizing it, they were already introducing themselves as a couple. Things seemed to be working, even if they were still in the early stages—getting to know each other, exploring the growing intimacy between them.

But eventually, they reached a point where neither could imagine a day without the other. What had started with a few tentative texts and casual dates had blossomed into something deeper. Something real.

And then, one special night over candlelight, the moment neither had spoken of—but both had felt—finally arrived.

"I think I'm in love with you," Jim said, his voice steady, but laced with vulnerability.

Lori looked at him for a long moment, as if imprinting every word onto her heart. Then, with a smile that outshone the candles between them, she replied:

"I feel the same."

And in that moment, Jim knew—with absolute certainty—that she meant it. The feeling was mutual.

Dimitri, who had seen it coming long before they admitted it, wasn't the least bit surprised. His intuition—and experience—had already told him everything he needed to know. The signs had been crystal clear: Jim and Lori were in love. And the best part? Jim had stopped trying to hide it. In fact, he embraced it with quiet pride.

So much so that one day, he walked up to Dimitri with a request that said more than words ever could.

"Dimitri, I need your wisdom on something… Would you help me pick out an engagement ring, my friend?"

Dimitri paused, eyeing him for a moment, as if making sure he'd heard correctly. Then a small chuckle slipped out, followed by a wide, knowing smile—as though everything in the universe had just clicked into place.

"For Lori?" he asked with playful mischief, clearly already knowing the answer but relishing the moment.

Jim arched an eyebrow and shot back,

"No, for that nice lady in the park…" he said dryly, before adding with a grin, "Of course for Lori! Who else?"

Dimitri burst out laughing, and without missing a beat, clapped Jim on the shoulder with a solid, brotherly thump—one that said everything words couldn't.

"You don't even have to ask," he replied between laughs, his voice full of warmth. He felt a deep sense of pride and joy in being part of such meaningful step in his friend's life. It was the kind of moment only true friends got to share—and one neither of them would ever forget.

Naturally, Jim had already introduced Lori to his parents during a cozy family gathering one afternoon. Selena and Conor were instantly taken with her, and it didn't take long for Lori to realize that Jim had wildly exaggerated when he'd described his mother as a prim, uptight, and strict Londoner. The reality couldn't have been more different.

To Lori, Jim's parents were absolutely delightful. Conor was warm and easy-going, always attentive, and eager to make guests feel welcome, while Selena turned out to be the embodiment of grace and kindness—sweet, affectionate, and naturally elegant, without even a hint of coldness or formality.

Later that evening, after Jim had driven her home, Lori smiled warmly as she said goodbye:

"I loved your parents—they're amazing. And your mum? She's nothing like your said! Not the least bit uptight or strict—she's charming, elegant, and so kind."

Jim burst out laughing, feigning outrage.

"That's because it's you! With us, it was a whole different story. 'Yes, ma'am! At your command, Sergeant!'" he said, throwing a mock salute and striking a stiff military pose before laughing again.

In truth, he'd always known his mother was loving—she just had a firm way of teaching manners, refinement, and good values.

Lori was welcomed into the O'Hara family with open arms, and the warmth she felt from them made her feel at home from the very start.

It was a bright, peaceful May day when, by sheer chance, Jim spotted Lori standing on a corner of Central Park. She seemed to be waiting for her group of tourists, whom she had let wander off for a bit—hopefully without getting lost! One by one, they were beginning to trickle back and gather around her.

Jim and Dimitri walked over to say hello, catching her pleasantly off guard.

"Good morning!" they greeted in unison, smiling.

"Oh! Hi—good morning!" Lori replied, clearly surprised, but genuinely happy to see them.

As they chatted casually, Lori continued to greet the returning tourists, counting them mentally as they reappeared. A few were still missing, but most were already back. That's when Dimitri, with his natural charm, addressed the group.

"Where are you from?" he asked with a warm smile.

"From Hawaii!" a few of them chimed in, clearly delighted by the friendly attention from the two officers.

Jim grinned, exchanging a quick look with Dimitri before turning back to the group.

"Well then—*Aloha!*[1] *E Komo Mai*[2]..." he said, carefully attempting the pronunciation, enjoying the curious looks he received. "Welcome to New York!" he added with a cheerful nod.

"*Mahalo*[3]!" they all responded in unison, clearly delighted and smiling warmly at Jim with genuine appreciation.

Lori looked at him too—wide-eyed, impressed by how effortlessly he spoke the Hawaiian phrase. Dimitri, though slightly surprised, wasn't at all shocked. He already knew Jim had an incredible gift for adapting to any situation, no matter how unexpected.

After a short pause, Jim's voice took on a more serious, almost secretive tone. He turned toward Lori with a meaningful look and a mis-

---

[1]   *Aloha* is a Hawaiian greeting that conveys not only *hello*, but also *peace*, *love*, and *affection*.

[2]   *E Komo Mai* means *welcome* in the Hawaiian language.

[3]   *Mahalo* is the Hawaiian word for *thank you*.

chievous wink, then shifted his gaze to the group of tourists…

"If you'll allow me a moment… I'd like you all to witness something very special," he said, eyes gleaming. "But let's wait for the rest of the group to return first."

Lori blinked at him, intrigued. *What on earth is he up to?*

The conversation flowed easily while the group waited, and one by one, the last of the tourists rejoined the circle. Lori did a quick count. All present. Just as she opened her mouth to give the signal to continue the tour, Jim exchanged a knowing glance with Dimitri. He already had his phone out, ready to capture the moment. With a wink, he gave Jim the go-ahead.

Then, completely unexpectedly, Jim stepped in front of Lori. His expression shifted to one of quiet seriousness, though the joy shining in his eyes was unmistakable. Without a word, he slowly dropped to one knee, his movements deliberate, as if every second mattered. A collective gasp rippled through the group as he pulled out a small, velvet-covered, heart-shaped box—something he'd been carrying with him all this time, waiting for the perfect moment. He opened it, revealing a breathtaking engagement ring that caught the sunlight, sparkling like the promise of a future together.

The Hawaiian tourists, now fully caught up in the moment, let out a loud, collective *"Ooooooh!"* of excitement and awe.

Lori stood frozen; her breath caught in her throat. Her eyes widened in shock as she stared at him, stunned. *Was this really happening? Here? Now? In front of all her tourists?* She couldn't believe it.

Then, with a voice filled with warmth and quiet certainty, Jim looked up at her and said:

"Lorraine Kiloha… will you marry me? Will you be my partner, my heart, my home?"

Tears welled up in Lori's eyes. She didn't know whether to laugh or cry—or both. The surprise had left her speechless, but the happiness blooming inside her was far too big to hide. This moment—unexpected, beautiful, and completely heartfelt—was everything.

"Yes!… Of course, I will!" she exclaimed, her voice full of euphoria. "Jim… yes…" she repeated, moved, her eyes brimming with love as she gazed at him.

Her group of tourists erupted into applause and cheers. The shouts of "Bravo!" and "Congratulations!" mingled with laughter and excited exclamations. Without missing a beat, they all began chanting together, full of enthusiasm:

"Go on, kiss! Go on, kiss!"

Dimitri, amused, let out a loud whistle as passers-by, catching sight of the scene, spontaneously joined in the applause.

Jim stood up, beaming, and without releasing Lori's hand, he pulled her toward him. Without a second thought, and amid laughter and happy tears, they shared a passionate kiss that sealed that magical, unexpected moment.

That corner of Central Park, for one brief moment, had become a stage for joy and celebration. And in the midst of it all, Jim and Lori both knew that this day would be forever etched in their hearts. Not to mention the pictures Dimitri was taking!

From that moment onward, they were officially engaged. What Jim didn't know at the time—though he found out later in the day—was that this day also happened to be Lori's 30th birthday, turning the occasion into a double celebration.

At the end of the day, after finishing their shifts, Jim and Dimitri invited Lori to join them for a champagne toast at their usual pub, of course, once she had finished her shift as well. Amid jokes and laughter, Jim was surprised to learn that he was eleven years older than Lori, something he had never thought much about. He had just turned 41, coincidentally in the same month as her: he on May 12th and she on the 27th.

Another curious coincidence came up during the conversation: Lory and her twin sister were both Gemini, which sparked even more jokes and laughter. But amid the fun, a fleeting concern crossed Jim's mind. He ran a hand through his hair and, with a mock expression of worry, said:

"Man, I feel old!"

His dramatic tone sent Lori and Dimitri into fits of laughter, and Dimitri, not missing a beat, slapped Jim on the back and shot back sarcastically:

"Come on, don't exaggerate. If you're old, I should be in a museum."

Lori, surprised to find out Jim's age, stared at him with wide eyes.

"Wow! I thought you were about my age. You definitely don't look it, Jim!" she exclaimed, completely sincere.

Jim smiled, clearly flattered by the compliment, and winked at her with a mischievous glint in his eye.

"Thanks, sweetheart. You're a real charmer," he said, laughing as he took her hand with tenderness.

"She's right, Jim. You do look like a kid…" Dimitri joked, laughing heartily, though he meant it with a genuine fondness. "But honestly, age is just a number. When there's true love, it doesn't matter at all. And you're both of legal age!" he added with a playful grin, winking at them both.

Raising his glass, Dimitri added with a touch of pride:

"I'm ten years older than my wife, and here we are, still going strong after all these years. We've raised five kids with love and respect, and that age difference never made a bit of difference."

His words seemed to dissolve any lingering doubts Jim had. Looking at Lori, smiling softly as they clinked glasses, Jim knew, without a doubt, that the only thing that mattered was what they shared with each other.

Now that they were officially engaged, their conversation naturally drifted toward the wedding. They began to envision what it would be like—the setting, the atmosphere, and the people who would be there to share their special day.

Jim had always enjoyed the idea of a big wedding, though he'd also considered the charm of a small, intimate one. Ultimately, he didn't mind which one it was—as long as it was with the right person. Still, he couldn't ignore the size of his family or the many friends who would want to celebrate with them. He didn't want to disappoint anyone. As much as he longed for something more private, he was starting to realize their wedding would likely need to be something grand.

Lori, on the other hand, didn't have strong preferences. As a child, like most little girls, she had once dreamed of a fairy-tale wedding with her prince charming waiting at the altar. She was excited about the idea of a big, beautiful ceremony, but she'd be just as happy with something smaller and more personal. After all, her family was small, though she had lots of friends. So, she left the decision to Jim.

The topic of religion quickly surfaced. Jim, being of Irish decent, was Catholic, while Lori, though she believed in God, didn't follow a particular faith. Her mother had grown up in a Mormon family, but after marrying her Christian Hawaiian father, they had agreed that love mattered more than their doctrinal differences. *"God is one and doesn't distinguish between creeds,"* they'd often said.

Fortunately, her family had never imposed any expectations on that front, so when it came time to choose the type of ceremony, they decided on a Catholic wedding. They respected Jim's family tradition, but more than anything, they knew that what truly mattered was the union itself, not the ritual that sealed it.

For now, it was just a conversation—an exchange of thoughts on the pros and cons of uniting their lives before God. But one thing was clear to both of them: they were believers, and beyond the grandness of the ceremony, what truly mattered was the commitment they were willing to make to each other.

They discussed choosing a meaningful date for their wedding, one that would add even more symbolic value to their union. Valentine's Day, the quintessential celebration of love, seemed like a lovely option. However, the following year, Valentine's Day would fall on a Sunday, and they didn't think it was entirely suitable since many of their guests would have to wake up early for work the next day.

Easter, with its profound spiritual significance, was another option they considered. It was also a beautiful time of the year for a wedding. Yet, in the end, they found a date even more unforgettable—one that represented love, family, hope, and the exchange of gifts: Christmas.

That year, Christmas Eve, their favourite day of the year, fell on a Friday, and although they had hoped to marry on that day, Christmas Day, which fell on a Saturday, also felt perfect. The idea immediately excited them. Getting married at Christmas felt like the most perfect gift—a way to seal their love on a magical, meaningful date.

They could have waited until the following year, when Christmas Eve would fall on a Saturday, but the truth was they didn't want to wait that long. The excitement of sharing such a momentous occasion led them to believe there was no better time than that Christmas.

Lori also suggested getting married in Hawaii. When she mentioned it to her parents, they were thrilled by the idea of celebrating the wedding in their homeland, surrounded by tropical beaches and the warm essence of the islands. They eagerly offered to organize everything, promising a truly authentic Hawaiian wedding—exotic, colourful, and filled with folkloric traditions that would make the event unforgettable.

To make it even more special, it would have a unique Christmas-Hawaiian twist! Picture lights twinkling between the palm trees, *leis* (flower garlands) adorned with festive touches, and the magic of Christmas blending with the aloha spirit, creating an enchanting and unforgettable atmosphere.

The reception, likely at sunset, would be a true *luau*—traditional music, hula dances, and a feast of island delicacies under a starlit sky. The warmth and joy of Hawaii would frame the celebration, making it as joyous as it was memorable.

The idea thrilled Jim as well, and for a moment, both of them were carried away by the dreamy vision of exchanging vows with the ocean as their witness and the tropical breeze gently embracing them, in a setting that was both magical and deeply meaningful to Lori.

However, after weighing the pros and cons, they realized that getting married so far away would pose a challenge for most of their loved ones. Most of their friends and family lived in New York, and many simply wouldn't be able to travel to Hawaii for various reasons—some of them quite obvious.

Ultimately, they chose what mattered most: celebrating their wedding surrounded by their closest family and friends. New York became the natural choice, where winter would lend an enchanting quality to the day, and with a little luck, snow would transform their celebration into a scene straight out of a fairy tale.

Being near family and friends also ensured that no one would miss the event. Lori's parents, in particular, were more than willing to travel, which made the decision easier and allowed them to focus on what was truly important: cherishing the moment.

However, they faced a considerable challenge: planning a wedding in just six months, as June was fast approaching. Still, they felt confident that the time was enough to meticulously organize every detail, from the ceremony to the celebration. They knew that love could overcome anything, and they were determined to make the day unforgettable.

The date would be magical, bathed in the warmth of Christmas, with twinkling lights, a beautifully decorated tree, carols in the air, and the loving presence of those who mattered most. A day of joy, gifts, and most importantly, the exchange of vows. Their "I do" would be the most precious gift—a bond that would last forever, sealed by their sincere and heartfelt promises.

Soon after, they began to dream about their honeymoon. Where would they go? They wanted a destination that was romantic, elegant, and truly embodied the essence of their love. While places like Thailand and tropical islands were popular among couples, they weren't interested in following trends. They wanted a location that truly reflected their unique relationship.

Hawaii, of course, came to mind. After all, it was Lori's home, a place rich with memories and significance for her. However, after some reflection, they realized that they could always visit it on holidays throughout their life together. For their honeymoon, they wanted something new—an experience unlike anything else to mark the beginning of their life as a married couple.

After much thought, they both agreed that the perfect choice would be two of the most iconic and romantic cities in the world: Paris and Rome. The timeless elegance of Paris, with its lights and artistic soul, and the majestic charm of Rome, with its ancient history and beauty, offered the ideal backdrop for their honeymoon.

Depending on how many days they could take off from work, they would plan to savour the best of both destinations. They would wander through the bohemian streets of Montmartre, toast with champagne beneath the Eiffel Tower, and enjoy a sunset cruise on the Seine. Then, in Rome, they would stroll through the ruins of the ancient city, toss a coin in the Trevi Fountain, and embrace the allure of "la dolce vita."

More than just a trip, it would be the ultimate celebration of their love in two of the world's most romantic cities, where every street corner, every moment, would create lasting memories.

Both of them had always dreamed of visiting Paris and Rome, and now they would get to do it together, as newlyweds. That realization only deepened their certainty that they were truly made for each other. They were soulmates.

During their engagement, they dove headfirst into the wedding preparations. The first priority was finding the perfect church. Jim was certain about where and who could marry them; his only concern was whether the chosen date, December 25th, would be available.

They reached out to their friend, Father Bob[4], a charismatic and unconventional Catholic priest with a great sense of humour. He was the pastor of a small, welcoming church that felt more like a chapel, tucked away among the towering

---

[4]   You can discover Father Bob's full story in my novel, *In God's Hands.*

skyscrapers of Brooklyn. The church's name held deep significance: The Portal of Heaven.

When they proposed the idea, Father Bob was overjoyed. Luckily, he had no prior commitments that afternoon, as his only Christmas Mass was scheduled for noon. He also eagerly accepted their invitation to the reception, admitting that he absolutely loved weddings—and to the surprise of many—he was an excellent dancer!

With the church secured, their next task was to find a venue for the reception and party. However, organizing an event during the holiday season posed its challenges. Still, they faced each obstacle with excitement, knowing that every step brought them closer to the day they would unite their lives.

As the planning continued, they also made sure to carve out time to enjoy each other's company. They spent their days off having picnics in Central Park, sharing long conversations, laughter, and stolen moments of affection over glasses of wine. They loved dancing, dining out, and strolling in the rain—small pleasures that both cherished and that made them feel like the leading characters in their own love story. From time to time, they escaped to nearby spots for weekend getaways, creating memories they would hold dear forever. Their romance was nothing short of magical.

One afternoon, they had planned to have a picnic in Central Park. Jim picked her up, and before heading to the park, she insisted on making a quick stop at a nearby supermarket to grab a few more treats. While she was inside, he waited on a bench, the picnic basket beside him, already prepared: a bottle of wine with glasses, delicate canapés, freshly made sandwiches, and a cozy blanket to sit on the grass.

Before long, he saw her returning, a radiant smile lighting up her face, a bag in her hand.

"We forgot the champagne!" she exclaimed with a joyful laugh, holding up the bottle like a treasure just found.

Unable to resist, Jim leaned in and gave her a quick kiss. "What would I do without you? You think of everything!" he said, swept up in her enthusiasm. Together, they walked to find the perfect spot, tucked beneath the shade of a large tree.

They settled on the blanket, enjoying the soft breeze and the distant hum of the city. Jim's gaze never left her, mesmerized. Then, something shifted in him. He couldn't quite place it, but there was a change, a subtle difference. She still looked beautiful, playful as always, but something was off—something that didn't quite fit. He couldn't explain it, but a strange sensation swept through him.

Noticing his inquisitive stare, she flashed him a mischievous smile.

"What's wrong?" she asked gently.

Jim hesitated for a moment before responding.

"I don't know…" he chuckled softly. "You seem… different."

"Different?" she repeated, arching a playful eyebrow. "In what way?"

He studied her closely, trying to put his finger on the odd feeling.

"I'm not sure," he laughed, scratching the back of his neck. "Maybe it's just the afternoon light, but… it's like you're not really you."

Before he could say anything more, a burst of laughter rang out behind him. He turned quickly, his expression shifting from confusion to shock as he saw… another Lori? She was walking toward him, laughing uncontrollably, as if this were the funniest thing in the world.

Jim blinked, stunned. Then he turned his gaze back to the woman sitting in front of him, and everything clicked.

It wasn't Lori. It was Lily!

The twins had swapped places as soon as Lori went to the supermarket, intending to see if Jim would notice the difference between them.

At first, Jim was baffled. He never would have suspected they would pull such a trick on him, but soon his confusion melted into laughter. What amazed him most was that, despite the fact that Lily and Lori were identical, something inside him told him this woman wasn't his Lori.

And that realization changed everything. Because, without quite understanding how, he recognized her. His heart knew. It wasn't about a physical detail or an obvious difference. It was her energy, her gaze, her very essence. Jim knew Lori so intimately that, even though her twin was her exact reflection, his soul was telling him this wasn't her.

Lori walked up to him and kissed him on the cheek, still laughing, but with a gleam of joy in her eyes, knowing that he had figured it out. It felt like a playful game between soulmates.

"Well, Jim..." said Lily, winking at him. "I must admit, we didn't fool you. Congratulations, you noticed!"

Jim looked back and forth between Lily and Lori, and in an instant, all three of them burst into laughter, celebrating the clever and successful prank.

"Of course I noticed," Jim murmured, intertwining his fingers with Lori's. "Because now I know for certain—we are soulmates."

She squeezed his hand affectionately, and in that moment, they both knew with unwavering certainty that nothing and no one could ever confuse their love.

Whenever Lily was home on leave, Lori took full advantage of the opportunity to move forward with the wedding preparations. Shopping for the wedding and bridesmaids' dresses was a top priority, and Lily, being her identical twin, was the perfect companion for those moments.

But they weren't alone in this adventure. Jim's sister, Nicky, also joined in whenever she had time off, and together they made an inseparable team. The three of them had become fast friends from the very beginning, and each shopping trip quickly turned into the perfect excuse for sharing laughter, toasts, and stories. More than just sisters-in-law, they felt like real sister.

As for Jim, he wasn't alone in his mission either. In addition to having his best friend, Dimitri, as his partner in crime, he also had his younger brother, Andy, by his side, who was thrilled to accompany him in choosing his wedding suit and the outfits for the groomsmen.

Each group experienced the excitement in their own way: the women, surrounded by dresses, veils, and accessories, dreaming about the big day, and the men, navigating through suits, drinks, and jokes, enjoying the camaraderie of male bonding.

These were truly special moments, filled with friendship, joy, and mutual understanding. Even though they each moved forward with the preparations separately, they all shared the joy of creating an unforgettable memory together.

Between their work schedules and the whirlwind of wedding planning, time seemed to fly by.

Yet, amid the whirlwind of emotions and responsibilities, Lori received news she had long been waiting for. Something she had deeply hoped for, and when it came, it took her by surprise—but in the sweetest way possible. Everything seemed to be falling into place, as though destiny were smiling on her with every step.

She was on cloud nine! She couldn't wait to share the news with Jim, but she wanted to make it special. So that night, when they went out for dinner, she decided to wait for the perfect moment.

When dessert arrived, with her heart pounding, she took a deep breath, and with a radiant smile, she excitedly said:

"Jim, honey…"—her eyes sparkling with happiness—"I just got a call from Hawaiian Airlines… They've accepted me for training!"

Lori could hardly contain her joy. She'd sent her CV, along with all the necessary documents and requirements for the airline, some time ago, and finally, the wait had paid off. She had dreamed of this moment for months, imagining how it would feel to receive that call. Now, becoming a flight attendant was one step closer to becoming her reality. Jim, fully aware of what this achievement meant to her, and all the interviews, tests, and challenges she had overcome to get here, paused for a moment, processing the news. Then, a huge smile lit up his face. With a burst of excitement, he stood up, raised his champagne glass, and, without hesitation, took her hand, inviting her to join him.

"This calls for a toast, my love! You did it! Congratulations!"

They clinked glasses, and before Lori could react, Jim kissed her passionately right there, indifferent to the curious gazes of the other diners.

Seeing this, many in the restaurant began clapping, assuming they had just gotten engaged.

Amid laughter, Jim pulled back slightly, beaming with pride, and announced loudly:

"My girl is going to be a flight attendant!"

Some, surprised, asked, "For what airline?" "Hawaiian Airlines!" she replied, glowing with happiness.

The applause erupted once again, and Lori, both flustered and overwhelmed with emotion, thanked the kind strangers who celebrated with them. Without a doubt, that night would remain forever etched in her memory as another magical moment in their love story.

Two weeks later, after submitting her resignation with the proper notice, Lori said goodbye to her job as a tour guide. Although she felt a sense of nostalgia, as she was well-liked at the travel agency, her colleagues and supervisors understood that this was simply another step in her journey.

They had known for quite some time that her true passion was to become a flight attendant, and that this moment, sooner or later, would come. So, while the farewell was filled with heartfelt hugs and warm wishes, no one was truly surprised—rather, they were happy for her.

On her final shift, the agency threw her a small farewell party with balloons, cake, and a card signed by all her coworkers, wishing her the best of luck on her new adventure. Lori was deeply touched and grateful for the love and kindness she had received, as well as for the wonderful friends she had made along the way.

With her heart full of excitement and her suitcase packed with dreams, she would soon begin her training as a flight attendant with Hawaiian Airlines. This meant she would need to relocate to Honolulu for at least six weeks to complete the required course.

During that time, Jim and she would be apart, perhaps even longer, until she was assigned to a route—ideally on the New York-Hawaiian flights, or based at the New York hub, possibly in Terminal 4 at JFK, where she had requested to work. Despite the distance, a new chapter of her life was unfolding, and she couldn't be more thrilled.

LORI, FLIGHT ATTENDANT

AFTER A HEARTFELT goodbye and a passionate kiss at JFK Airport, Lori boarded her flight to Honolulu, Hawaii. With her parents living there, she didn't have to worry about where to stay—she'd be going home.

Coming home was deeply emotional. It had been a while since they'd last seen each other, and the reunion was full of warmth and tenderness. Her parents were waiting at the Honolulu International Airport, arms wide open, hearts brimming with pride. They knew just how much this journey meant to her. From the time she was little, Lori had dreamed of becoming a flight attendant. Now, at last, she was taking a major step toward making that dream a reality.

They also knew about her engagement to Jim, whom they'd already met over video calls. The couple was deep into wedding planning, which made Lori's homecoming even more special. For her parents, seeing their daughter return—ready to start her training with Hawaiian Airlines and looking ahead to a life with Jim—was a moment of pure joy.

The love and support of her family helped ease the ache of being away from Jim. Her parents welcomed her with open arms and encouraging words. The distance was hard, yes—but being surrounded by family gave her the strength she needed.

And once training began, Lori barely had time to dwell on the separation. She threw herself into the experience, staying so busy and so focused that time seemed to fly. To her delight, she was having the time of her life.

From the very first day, they were asked to wear their eye-catching uniforms. The women could choose between a solid-coloured dress or a floral-print blouse paired with a skirt or trousers. The men wore trousers and matching floral-print shirts. Wearing the full uniform helped them get used to working in it, just as they would on duty.

Lori loved every part of her flight attendant training. They started with the basics—even the things that seemed almost silly at first, like how to walk, how to carry themselves, how to be kind and efficient. But every detail mattered. The classes were dynamic, fun, and engaging, turning what could have been a daunting process into a truly rewarding experience.

As the training progressed, the lessons took a practical turn—they began flying on actual aircrafts. Taking turns in each session, sometimes as passengers and sometimes as flight attendants, they were able to apply what they had learned in a real-world setting. Experiencing an actual flight allowed them to put their skills into practice, making the training not only exciting but also fully immersive and authentic.

One of the most unusual topics they covered was how to respond if a passenger gave birth mid-flight. While such situations are rare—since women in the later stages of pregnancy are generally not permitted to fly—there are exceptions. That's why it was essential to be prepared for the unexpected and to know how to handle such a rare, yet potentially critical, emergency. After all, you never know when you might need to help bring a baby into the world... right there in the aisle of a plane!

The sixth and final week of training was dedicated entirely to onboard safety and emergency management. Participants received instruction on evacuation protocols, the use of emergency equipment, and administering first aid in critical situations. They also learned how to manage crises during a flight—from severe turbulence to possible passenger incidents—developing the skills to stay calm, reassure travellers, and respond quickly and effectively no matter the circumstances.

During the lively sessions, they also learned a few basic words in Hawaiian—something Lori already knew well. Being Hawaiian and having studied in Hawaii, she was already fluent. For her, those words were a comforting reminder of home. For most of her classmates, however, it was a way to feel more connected to the local culture—a small but meaningful gesture that made them feel even more part of the Hawaiian Airlines team.

After one final exam to assess everything they had learned, the trainees received their results. Shortly afterward, they began receiving their flight route assignments. However, these initial placements were not permanent, and they had to be ready to operate various routes depending on demand. While trainees could indicate their preferred route, priority was generally given to senior flight attendants.

Lori was provisionally assigned to the central base in Honolulu, and her very first official flight was a short route—just 40 minutes long.

Her first official day began at the crack of dawn. With a flight scheduled to depart at 6:00 a.m., Lori had to arrive early—flawless and composed, with perfectly styled hair and a touch of natural makeup applied with care. As part of the Hawaiian Airlines uniform, each female flight attendant wore a flower tucked behind one ear.

According to tradition, a woman places the flower on the left side if she's married, and on the right if she's single and open to love. Though fewer people take the symbolism seriously today, it remains a sweet tribute to Hawaiian culture.

Lori, though not yet married, was no longer searching—her heart already belonged to someone. Proudly, she placed the flower on the left side, embracing the role she would soon step into.

Her inaugural flight from Honolulu (HNL) to Maui (OGG) was set to land around 6:40 a.m., but the day wouldn't end there—several flights filled her schedule. For now, her routes were limited to the islands, allowing her to stay with her parents. While that offered comfort and warmth of home, her thoughts often drifted to Jim. She missed him more than she let on. Still, new recruits had little choice in their schedules or destinations—they had to accept what was assigned to them, at least until they built enough experience to request changes.

During that time apart, Jim and Lori experienced something unusual yet deeply comforting—a strange and profound sense of connection. It was as if they could feel what the other was going through, sense each other's moods, and sometimes even intuitively know if the other was feeling well. It was as though their hearts, minds, and even their souls were somehow synced—despite the physical distance.

Were they already practicing the vows they'd one day exchange? In sickness and in health… in distance and in closeness… Though miles apart, the flame of love between them—something only true soulmates share—continued to burn brightly. The invisible yet unbreakable bond they shared kept their connection alive, like a guiding light in the dark.

That time apart proved to be a true test of fire—a challenge that, rather than weakening them, only strengthened their love and deepened their commitment to one another.

Shortly after starting her job as a flight attendant—and even though she knew it was still early to make any formal requests—Lori decided to speak with her supervisors. She informed them of her upcoming wedding and expressed her desire to transfer to the New York base. She explained that her fiancé, Jim, worked as a police officer there, and that New York had already been her permanent residence before joining Hawaiian Airlines.

The company listened and promised to consider her request, though they couldn't give her an immediate answer. They knew the wedding was set for Christmas, and until then, she would have to stick with her current assignments and continue flying as scheduled. Still, they assured her that her wish to be transferred to New York would be considered and that she'd be informed as soon as a decision was made.

Lori was beyond happy to finally be living her dream of flying, but the distance form Jim was harder than she'd imagined. He missed her just as much, and they both worked to stay close despite the time zones and packed routines. They exchanged messages constantly and tried to talk every night before going to sleep, whenever their shifts allowed.

Her parents, Vincent and Gwendolyn Kiloha, offered her loving support and encouragement every step of the way. They had always believed in her and were proud of the woman she had become. But they also understood how bittersweet it was for her to finally reach her dream at a time when love had placed so many miles between her and the man she hoped to build a life with.

Still, they were optimistic that everything would work out. They had a quiet confidence that the airline would eventually grant her the transfer. In the meantime, wedding plans continued across the distance. Her parents were already preparing to fly with her to New York for the big day—an event they looked forward to with joy and anticipation.

Even so, Lori couldn't shake a few nerves. At one point, she even thought about postponing the wedding until the transfer was confirmed. But her parents reassured her. Christmas was a time of hope and magic, they reminded her, and everything would fall into place. Her father, Vincent Kiloha, held her hand gently and said:

"He Aloha Ke Akua" an old Hawaiian saying that means *"God is Love."*

And her mother, Gwendolyn, smiling sweetly, added:

"And when God steps in, no man can stop Him! That day will be perfect, sweetheart. Just have faith."

Then she kissed her on the forehead, passing on, with that simple gesture, all the calm and love in the world.

Even though Lori was filled with excitement, she still hadn't found the perfect wedding dress. She had visited boutiques in New York with her twin sister, Lily, and Jim's sister, Nicky, but none of the dresses she tried on seemed quite right. However, they had already chosen the bridesmaids' dresses, which were absolutely stunning—elegant, festive, and perfectly suited for the Christmas season.

That's when her mother, Gwen, decided to step in. Knowing Lori's indecisiveness and aware of the chilly New York weather, she suggested they go together to find a special, custom-made dress for the season. She knew a talented tailor who could create the ideal design just in time for the wedding.

Excited, mother and daughter embarked on a long-awaited shopping day—something they hadn't done in years, but this time with an even more special purpose: to pick out Lori's wedding dress. They visited bridal boutiques, examined fabrics, and explored designs, letting their excitement guide every decision. Between laughter and champagne toasts, they shared a truly unforgettable moment, one of those memories that would stay with them forever.

The only cloud on such a perfect day was Lily's absence, as she was away on a mission and couldn't join them. Still, there was no doubt that she would be there on the big day. As the maid of honour, alongside Nicky, she wouldn't miss it for anything.

The months flew by, and with each passing day, the wedding day drew closer. Jim and Lori yearned to be reunited. They missed seeing each other, touching, kissing, and hugging after so much time apart. Although Lori loved her job and thoroughly enjoyed every day of her island-hopping flights, she couldn't help but feel a growing sense of anxiety about not making it in time for her wedding to the love of her life, Jim.

What if her request was denied? Or, at the very least, what if she didn't get the necessary approval to ensure she could be there in time to marry him?

Then, in late October, Hawaiian Airlines offered her the chance to extend her training to operate in larger aircraft, such as the Airbus A330, which would qualify her for longer flights. Her superiors not only suggested this opportunity but highly recommended it, as it would open up new career prospects. Lori didn't hesitate for a second; for her, every new experience was another step in her professional development. She was eager to prepare herself for any type of aircraft and continue advancing in her career as a flight attendant.

After successfully completing the training and obtaining certification to operate wide-body aircraft, Lori finally received the long-awaited news at the beginning of November: starting in December, her new base would be at JFK Airport's Terminal 4 in New York.

She was over the moon with happiness. She had finally been assigned to New York… just in time for her wedding!

Her inaugural flight from Honolulu to New York was scheduled for November 30, and to her delight, her parents would be flying on that very flight. Excited and proud, they would have the chance to see her in action, performing with professionalism and elegance as a flawless flight attendant. They would also arrive early enough to help with the final wedding preparations, making the moment even more meaningful.

Lori's first flight to New York would be aboard an A330. It was Flight HA624, scheduled to depart from Honolulu (HNL) at 11:15 p.m. The itinerary included a one hour and 45-minute layover in San Francisco (SFO), with an arrival time of 7:20 the following morning. From San Francisco, she would resume her journey at 9:01 a.m., heading toward New York's International Airport (JFK), where she was expected to land at 5:41p.m. The entire trip would span approximately 12 hours and 26 minutes.

When Lori called Jim to share the news, their excitement was almost uncontrollable. After all the waiting, everything seemed to fall perfectly into place.

Upon arriving in New York, her parents made their way to the baggage claim while Lori remained on the plane to finish her final tasks. As a flight attendant, she had to inspect the cabin, make sure no passengers had left anything behind, and ensure everything was in order before she could say goodbye to the rest of the crew. Only then could she finally go meet her family.

The long journey and time zone change left her visibly tired, but the excitement of being reunited with Jim erased any trace of fatigue.

Though Jim, and Lori's parents had already met through several Skype video calls, this was the first time they would meet in person. They greeted each other warmly with hugs and smiles as they waited for Lori.

When Lori finally emerged with her small cabin suitcase bearing the Hawaiian Airlines logo, Jim could hardly contain himself. There she was, more beautiful than ever, walking straight toward him after months of waiting. Holding a large bouquet of flowers in one hand and a bright, radiant smile, he reached for her the moment she crossed into the arrival area. Ignoring the crowd of travellers and airport staff, he pulled her into his arms and kissed her passionately, as though time had paused just for them.

Before heading home, Lori still had one final task to complete: she needed to report to Terminal 4 at JFK, where she would begin her new base of operations. There, she would finalize the paperwork and receive her upcoming flight assignments, which were still to be confirmed.

This first step marked her official integration into the New York-based crew, bringing her one step closer to the life she's always dreamed of with Jim.

Jim drove them home, where Lori lived with her twin sister, Lily. However, due to her demanding job as a military nurse, Lily was often away and, at that moment, was overseas on a mission. She was expected to return in time for the wedding, though, and would finally be able to reunite with their parents after a long time apart.

During their stay in New York, Lori's parents would stay in the guest room, which was actually Lily's. For the occasion, the sisters would share a room again, a nostalgic delight that reminded them of their childhood when they would stay up late talking before falling asleep.

After ensuring Lori and her parents were settled and comfortable, Jim kissed her goodbye with love and headed to his home, as he had to work the next day. But this time, the goodbye was sweet, not bitter, because, at last, they were in the same city and would have many more chances to be together.

Lori eagerly embarked on her new chapter based in New York, thrilled to be closer to Jim, and take the next step in her career. While her assignments varied with each shift, the flights were now longer and more demanding, which meant extended periods of rest. Fortunately, this gave her the chance to spend more time with Jim, balancing the long hours of work with precious moments together.

As they both focused on their respective duties, they adapted and organized their schedules for their future together, adjusting routines and planning their life as a couple. The days seemed to fly by, and with the wedding day drawing near, Lori felt a mix of excitement and nerves. Every little detail that fell into place made their dream of marrying at Christmas feel more and more tangible.

Lori made it a habit to text Jim every time she landed—whether it was during a layover, in transit, or upon reaching her final destination. This gave him peace of mind, allowing him to follow her journey and know everything had gone smoothly. Despite the physical distance caused by their work schedules, they always found ways to stay connected, sharing small moments that made them feel close, no matter the miles between them.

After returning from one of her thrilling flights, Lori excitedly recounted an unusual incident she had experienced on board. Her eyes sparkled with enthusiasm as she described how everyone on board had witnessed something inexplicable in the sky.

"It looked like a massive upside-down fig, floating in the sky, bathed in a dazzling, pure white light—almost otherworldly… like angels were inhabiting it," Lori said, her voice filled with awe.

"It was amazing, Jim! Majestic, hypnotic… celestial!" she exclaimed, still in disbelief over the sight.

"I never really thought much about these things, but now I have no doubt… I saw a UFO, Jim!" Lori said, laughing with a mix of excitement and wonder, as though she couldn't quite process what she had witnessed.

Jim knew Lori wasn't one to fabricate stories, but still, he smiled, amused by her excitement. With a playful tone, he replied:

"Next time, take a picture—I want to see it too!" Jim exclaimed.

Lori, laughing, quickly pulled out her phone and showed him the photo. It was a bit blurry, but still unmistakable: a massive upside-down fig-shaped object, glowing with an intense, ethereal light that lit up the surrounding sunset clouds.

"Are you kidding? You think I'd miss such an opportunity?" she said, still buzzing with excitement. "I think everyone on board snapped photos."

She grinned, while Jim stared at the image in awe, wide-eyed. The photo seemed real… and incredible.

"You're one lucky girl, my love," he said, still absorbed in the screen. "Keep that picture safe… you never know when you'll need proof that this actually happened."

They both laughed, savouring the moment, while Lori replayed the strange but captivating sight in her mind.

Christmas was fast approaching, and with it, the mounting anticipation and nerves that came with knowing their wedding day was just around the corner. Yet, Lori and Jim remained calm, knowing they had everything ready. Together, they went over their to-do list, checking off each item with satisfaction. Each tick mark brought a wave of relief as they saw their plans coming together.

The church, the restaurant, the outfits (for both the groom, groomsmen, bride, and bridesmaids), the rings—and most importantly, their parents, who had clicked immediately upon meeting and had quickly become close friends. That had been a source of joy for the couple.

There was almost nothing left to do… just wait with excitement. As each day passed, their anticipation grew, and everything was falling into place for their big day.

The honeymoon was also completely planned: Paris and Rome, over eight days—exactly the dream destinations they had both dreamed of. All that was left was packing, but they knew they still had time for that. In the meantime, they focused on enjoying these last few days before their wedding, certain everything would go off without a hitch.

Lori still had a few flights to complete before the wedding and honeymoon days off—a full fortnight, a true privilege considering how little time she'd been with the company. Jim was lucky too; he got the same fifteen days off, ensuring they would overlap and allowing them to enjoy each moment together without rushing. They both counted down the days eagerly, ready to leave behind their routines and fully embrace their celebration of love.

FLIGHT HA4925

 before the wedding would take her from New York (JFK) to Seattle (SEA)—a 6-hour and 20-minute journey that would carry her from coast to coast. Her return was scheduled for Wednesday, on a flight that, thanks to favourable winds, would be noticeably shorter at just 5 hours and 10 minutes. That Wednesday would not only mark her last day on duty, but also the beginning of her time off—perfectly timed to coincide with Jim's. Starting Thursday, December 23, her thoughts would no longer be on flight schedules or passenger lists, but on the final details of their wedding.

Her last day off had been the previous Thursday, meaning she'd been working non-stop since Friday. On Tuesday morning, around 9:00 a.m., Jim drove her to the JFK Airport. Since his shift didn't start until noon, there was no rush, and they took their time—sharing a coffee and talking with the ease of two people trying to stretch every second, fully aware that in just a few hours, thousands of miles would be between them.

Sitting across from each other, hands intertwined on the table, they enjoyed the festive atmosphere around them. Both loved Christmas, and they couldn't help but comment on how beautiful everything looked—the city, the airport, and the world around them glowing with holiday lights and decorations.

As usual, Lori had to report well in advance for her 11:30 a.m. flight. Before saying goodbye—with a kiss full of promise—she honoured their little ritual: assuring him she'd call as soon as she landed in Seattle, before heading to the hotel.

According to the itinerary, her flight was scheduled to land in Seattle at 2:49 p.m. local time, which would be 5:49 p.m. in New York. She figured that, after checking the cabin to ensure no passenger had left anything behind, they would disembark and, after handling the usual post-flight formalities, she'd be able to call him between 6:30 and 7 p.m. New York time—just before heading to her accommodation.

Jim's shifts typically lasted around ten hours, starting at noon and ending at 10:00 p.m. However, they both knew that while his start time was set in stone, the end of his day wasn't always guaranteed—especially if an urgent case kept him longer.

Meanwhile, the hours passed, and Jim and Dimitri began their shift. Jim's mind couldn't help but drift to Lori. He knew he wouldn't see her until Thursday morning, when her flight was scheduled to land at 6:00 a.m. That would mark the official start of their wedding holidays. But what truly mattered to him was that, from that moment on, she'd be his—and his alone—for the next fortnight they had been granted for the occasion.

He did his best to stay focused—on the job, on Dimitri's easy humour—but the anticipation for six-thirty was impossible to ignore.

Jim found himself daydreaming about their honeymoon, imagining every little detail, as if doing so might make time move just a bit faster. Even so, he kept checking the clock. He knew there was a chance he'd be busy when her call came—his work could shift from calm to chaos in an instant—but at the very least, he hoped to see a message from her. He'd reply with one of his own, as they always did—sharing that private ritual of theirs, a kind of love letter in motion, a way of making love through words across the distance.

Once boarding was complete, everything unfolded with the precision of a well-rehearsed choreography. Lori and the rest of the crew greeted passengers with warm smiles and a friendly, "Welcome aboard." They assisted some with stowing their carry-on luggage in the overhead compartments and ensured that everyone was comfortably seated, with seatbacks upright and seatbelts fastened.

The flight wasn't completely full, with just over 60% occupancy. This meant the journey would likely be calmer than usual, without the constant rush that came with a packed aircraft. There might even be brief moments to breathe between services—something rare on busier routes.

Because of the lower passenger count, the crew was also smaller. Instead of the usual eight to ten flight attendants typically assigned to this type of aircraft, there were only six on board: two men and four women.

Once boarding was finished and the cabin secured for take-off, the plane departed on time, bound for Seattle.

As the aircraft taxied towards the runway, it was time for the safety demonstration. As with every flight, Lori and her colleagues walked the aisle with professionalism and patience, delivering safety instructions that many passengers either overlooked or found monotonous. They pointed out the emergency exits, demonstrated how to fasten and unfasten seatbelts, explained the procedure in case of cabin depressurization—when oxygen masks would drop automatically—and indicated where to find life vests in the event of a water landing. While some travellers found these briefings unnecessary or even unsettling, to the crew, they were essential—just as critical as any other part of their responsibilities.

Lori was lucky to be working her shift with Virgil, a flight attendant who, while not exactly a veteran, was the most experienced crew member on this flight. With his charming sense of humour, he could draw smiles from both passengers and fellow crew. His well-timed jokes and witty remarks lightened the mood in the cabin, making the journey more pleasant for everyone on board.

Not long after take-off, once the plane had reached cruising altitude, the captain's voice came through the intercom with practiced ease:

"Good morning, ladies and gentlemen. This is Captain Clyde Cummings speaking on behalf of the entire crew. Welcome aboard flight HA4925 with service to Seattle.

We're now cruising at an altitude of 33,000 feet and anticipating a smooth flight. The estimated duration is approximately six hours and thirty minutes, with favourable weather conditions expected along the route.

We invite you to sit back, relax, and enjoy the onboard service. If you need anything, our crew is here to assist you.

Thank you for choosing to fly with us. We wish you a pleasant journey."

Meanwhile, the crew began the refreshment service. Lori and her colleagues worked efficiently, offering drinks and snacks with friendly smiles, later coming back through the cabin to collect any trash and make sure every passenger was comfortable. From time to time, they walked up and down the aisle attentively, always ready to assist with any requests or needs that might arise.

After clearing away the remains of the service, Lori noticed a passenger gesturing to her hesitantly. His expression was uneasy, and when she approached, he lowered his voice as if he didn't want others to hear.

"Excuse me, miss. This might sound strange, but... before boarding, a man handed me this envelope and told me it had to reach the pilot. No matter what."

He extended the envelope toward her, visibly nervous, as if it were burning his hands.

Lori arched an eyebrow, her curiosity piqued. She took the envelope cautiously and examined it. It was completely blank—no markings, no name, nothing at all.

"Are you sure this was meant for the captain?" she asked, keeping her tone calm and steady.

The man nodded quickly, his voice firmer this time.

"That's what he said—it had to be delivered directly to the pilot."

"Did you know the man? Was he part of the crew?" Lori continued, hoping to gather more information.

The passenger shook his head and shrugged. "No, I didn't know him at all. And he didn't look like a crew member—he wasn't wearing a uniform. He was tall, dressed completely in black, and wore a cap with mirrored sunglasses. I barely saw his face! He was also wearing gloves… He didn't give me his name or any explanation."

He paused, then added in a near whisper: "Why did he give it to me? I don't understand…" he murmured, more to himself than to Lori.

She kept her gaze on the envelope for a moment longer before responding calmly.

"Thank you. I'll deliver it to the captain right away. If it's meant for him, he'll know what it's about."

She offered him a reassuring smile, trying not to alarm him. But in her mind, a question lingered: *Why all the secrecy?*

After briefing her colleague Virgil, Lori made her way to the cockpit. When she reached the door, she picked up the interphone handset and pressed the call button.

"Captain Cummings, it's Lori."

A soft click indicated the door had been unlocked from the inside. Lori stepped in with her usual smile and the envelope in hand.

"Sir, one of the passengers gave me this envelope. He said it had to be delivered to the pilot."

Before he could speak, the co-pilot Charles Monroe chuckled in an amused tone:

"Clyde, looks like you've got a secret admirer!"

The captain and Lori both laughed.

As the captain took the envelope with curiosity, Lori briefly explained the situation. Once finished, she adopted a lighter tone and asked kindly:

"Can I bring you coffee?"

The captain, still examining the envelope with interest, looked up and smiled.

"A good coffee is always appreciated. Thank you, Lori."

Beside him, Monroe grinned. "Count me in for one, too."

"Certainly! I'll be right back with your coffees," Lori replied, flashing a bright smile before exiting the cockpit, leaving the intrigued pilots behind with the mysterious envelope.

As soon as Lori exited the cockpit, Captain Cummings, driven by a surge of curiosity, immediately opened the envelope. Inside, he found a sheet of white paper with an anonymous message, printed in bold, black, capital letters. He read in silence, the air in the cockpit suddenly thickening with tension.

The message read:

FLIGHT COMMANDER OF HA4925: THERE IS A BOMB ON BOARD THAT WILL DETONATE BELOW 13,000 FEET.

Cummings blinked, stunned. He quickly read it again, making sure his eyes weren't deceiving him. His heart began to pound, but years of training kept him calm.

He passed the note to his co-pilot, Charles Monroe, who took it with a furrowed brow. As Monroe read the message, his expression tightened.

"What kind of joke is this?" Monroe muttered, though his voice held more concern than disbelief.

For a moment, the two men exchanged silent glances. Neither wanted to succumb to panic, but they both knew that if this was real, they were facing a grave situation.

"If this is a sick joke, it's in extremely poor taste..." Monroe said quietly, his eyes still fixed on the paper.

Cummings inhaled deeply, his mind racing.

They couldn't afford to second-guess.

"We need to contact New York air traffic control. And no one else finds out until we have a plan."

What had been a normal flight just moments ago had now turned into a potential emergency.

Captain Cummings stared at the note one more time, as though rereading it might reveal a clue that it was just a prank. But there was no room for doubt.

As he carefully folded the note and placed it in the tray under his seat, Monroe nodded seriously. Without wasting a moment, he began preparing to communicate with air traffic control. Just then, Lori knocked softly at the door, which they had left open, entering with the coffees. They weren't ready for anyone to know what was happening, so Monroe froze, hiding his growing anxiety.

Outside, the crew carried on with their duties, completely unaware of the looming threat hanging over them. Inside the cockpit, Lori placed a tray with coffees on a small ledge, her movements deliberate and measured.

"Here you go, gentlemen," she said with a warm smile, having no idea that the atmosphere in the cockpit had shifted in just those few seconds.

But Lori was both observant and intuitive. It didn't take her long to notice the tension etched on their faces. Her smile faltered.

"Everything okay, gentlemen?" she asked, watching them closely, still wearing a smile—though now it was more for show. She didn't want them to realize she was already starting to suspect something was wrong.

Cummings glanced at her with a quick smile as he reached for his cup.

"Thanks, Lori. Everything's fine."

Lori wasn't convinced. The expressions on the captain and co-pilot's faces were far too serious. Maybe she was overreacting, but her instincts told her something wasn't right.

The captain gave her a subtle nod, indicating she could leave.

She hesitated for a moment, tempted to press the issue. But in the end, she gave a polite nod and stepped out of the cockpit. Still, the uneasy feeling lingered.

Just as the door clicked shut behind her, Monroe opened the comm channel to the control tower.

"Control, this is flight HA4925. We have a possible threat on board. Repeat—possible threat on board."

The tension inside the cockpit was palpable. The response came almost instantly.

"HA4925, can you confirm the nature of the threat?"

Cummings keyed his mic.

"We received an anonymous note stating there's an explosive device on board. The message claims the bomb will detonate if we descend below 13,000 feet. We're currently maintaining cruising altitude. No system anomalies, no unusual activity reported," he explained, then added, "Control, it might be a sick joke… but we're not taking any chances."

A heavy silence followed before the control tower replied.

"Understood, HA4925. We're assessing the situation. Maintain current altitude and await further instructions. Do not alert the passengers unless absolutely necessary."

Cummings closed his eyes for a moment, letting the weight of the situation sink in. It wasn't just about staying in control—they also had to keep the crew steady and alert, making sure panic didn't take hold of the flight. Sooner or later, they would have to inform them, and how they delivered the news could make all the difference.

"Flight HA4925, can you confirm whether there are any concrete signs of danger, or does this appear to be a false alarm?"

"Control, we've detected no anomalies on board so far. No reports of suspicious behaviour or visible signs of a threat. That said, we're following all safety protocols and maintaining cruising altitude."

"Copy that, HA4925. We'll coordinate with ground control in Seattle to prepare for your arrival. Any necessary measures will be taken based on the situation at hand."

"Understood, ground control. We'll continue monitoring and report any changes."

"Received, HA4925. Stay vigilant and follow standard safety procedures. We'll remain in contact."

Cummings engaged the autopilot and handed control over to Monroe. After a final sweep of the instruments, he stood up with quiet determination, ready to conduct a personal inspection of the aircraft.

Just as he approached the cockpit door, Lori appeared to collect the coffee cups.

Out of discretion, she said nothing about the mysterious envelope—if the captain hadn't brought it up, it wasn't her place to ask.

Monroe gave her a polite smile, and Cummings, just before stepping out, offered Lori a reassuring smile and a quick wink.

"Going to stretch my legs and clear my head for a minute," he said casually.

She returned the smile, gathered the cups, and walked away at an easy pace.

Meanwhile, the captain made his way down to the cargo hold, moving with quiet caution. His eyes scanned every accessible corner as he checked compartments, luggage areas, and any space where something suspicious could be hidden.

The thought of tearing through every suitcase was out of the question, and anyway, it would take hours, and time wasn't on their side.

After a thorough yet fruitless inspection, Cummings returned to the cockpit, a faint crease between his brows. He sank back into his seat and let out a discreet breath before glancing at Monroe.

"Nothing out of the ordinary," he said quietly. "If there's something on board, it's hidden—and hidden well."

Monroe nodded, understanding his colleague's frustration. They both knew they couldn't afford to get lost in speculation without concrete evidence. For a few moments, silence settled over the cockpit, broken only by the steady hum of the engines.

Eventually, they pushed the matter from their minds. There was nothing more they could do for now—not until it was time to begin their descent and prepare for landing. Only then would they discover whether the threat had been a grim joke or something far more real.

The flight continued smoothly. Outside the windows, the scenery slowly transformed—the East Coast was long behind them now, replaced by vast plains and majestic mountain ranges stretching far below. They had already covered nearly half the journey. In just over three hours, they would touch down in Seattle.

For Lori, this wasn't just another flight. It was one of the last before she stepped away from the skies for a while, to fully immerse herself in something even more meaningful: her upcoming wedding to Jim.

She felt content—fulfilled both professionally and personally. Flying was still a passion, but with each passing mile, she was also getting closer to a new chapter, one she embraced with joyful anticipation.

As the plane passed over Montana, it encountered a patch of strong turbulence, jolting the cabin and sparking murmurs of unease among the passengers. Some clutched their armrests; others exchanged anxious glances. But for Lori and the rest of the crew, it was all part of the job.

Moving calmly through the aisles, Lori and her teammates offered reassuring smiles, checking on passengers and reminding them that turbulence was a normal, temporary part of flying. Virgil, with his trademark sense of humour, began sharing exaggerates stories and spontaneous jokes, earning a few laughs, and easing the tension. His gift for turning discomfort into entertainment helped the passengers relax little by little.

When the turbulence finally passed and the plane levelled out, calm returned to the cabin. With just over two hours left until landing, the crew continued to keep spirits high, especially for those passengers weighed down by fatigue or nerves, eager to reach their destination.

A short wile later, Monroe left the cockpit to stretch his legs and make a quick stop at the restroom. On his way back, he quietly asked one of the flight attendants to gather the crew near the cockpit—Captain Cummings had something important to share.

No one suspected anything. Within minutes, the crew had gathered near the cockpit door, exchanging quiet remarks with the ease of those expecting a routine update. The mood remained light, unaware of the tension lingering just beyond the closed door.

Suddenly, the cockpit door opened, and Captain Cummings stepped out to meet the group. His expression was firm and composed, but there was a seriousness in his eyes that didn't go unnoticed by the more observant among them.

The curtains separating the cockpit from the rest of the aircraft were carefully drawn, ensuring that passengers couldn't see what was happening behind them. At a glance, everything appeared normal: the flight attendants stood in a circle, listening attentively to the captain, as if awaiting routine instructions. But what he was about to say would change the course of the flight entirely.

"I need your full attention," he said in a grave tone. "We've received a bomb threat on board. The details are unclear, and it may very well be a cruel hoax—but we must treat it with the utmost seriousness."

The group exchanged silent, tense glances.

Lori looked at the captain with a questioning gaze and, unable to help herself, asked,

"That envelope?" Cummings gave a slow nod.

"What are our next steps?" asked Virgil, keeping his composure.

"Search the aircraft for anything out of place or any suspicious packages. Do it discreetly—don't alarm the passengers. If you find anything unusual, don't touch it. Alert me immediately."

The flight attendants nodded and dispersed throughout the cabin, moving professionally through the aisles as if they were simply checking for cleanliness and order. They inspected the overhead compartments, unoccupied seats, lavatories, and storage areas.

Although all of them had been trained to handle emergencies, facing a real threat onboard was something else entirely. To make matters worse, there was no Air Marshal on this flight—those undercover agents who, on most flights—especially American ones—act as the last line of defence in such situations.

Without the support of a professional trained for this kind of crisis, they were on their own. And the only thing they could do now was stay calm, follow protocol, and hope the captain found a solution before the plane had to begin its descent.

After a thorough inspection, the crew returned one by one, each with the same report: nothing suspicious had been found.

Cummings nodded briefly, masking any hint of frustration. The threat remained unconfirmed, but it couldn't be dismissed either. His focus was clear: remain calm and adhere to protocol until they touched down in Seattle.

The flight continued as if nothing were wrong. Everything seemed routine, and the bomb threat lingered only as a quiet, unsettling possibility.

Montana was now far behind them, and they had long since passed the halfway point of their journey. Toward the back of the plane, Virgil, Lori, and two other crew members were speaking in low voices, doing their best to maintain a calm atmosphere while quietly discussing the situation. So far, there had been no sign of anything unusual, but the tension was still there—just beneath the surface.

"God, I hope this is just some twisted prank," Lori muttered, arms crossed. "That we land in Seattle, no drama, and no one ever has to find out."

"Yeah," another crew member replied, her tone measured but serious. "But we can't relax until we're on the ground."

Before the conversation could continue, the soft chime of a passenger call button interrupted them.

"I've got it," Lori said, straightening up.

She walked down the aisle toward the seat of the passenger who had pressed the button. He appeared to be in his early thirties, but something about him immediately raised a red flag—his skin was pale, his eyes sunken with dark circles, and a fine sheen of sweat coated his forehead.

"How can I help you, sir?" Lori asked with her usual kindness, though a flicker of concern had already crept into her expression.

The man swallowed hard before speaking, his voice unsteady.

"Just… a little water, please."

Lori returned quickly with a small bottle and a cup, but as she looked at him more closely, her worry deepened.

"Are you feeling all right?" she asked gently, leaning in slightly to get a better look.

The man let out a weak, nervous laugh.

"I think so. Just a sharp pain in my side… but it's easing up. Thanks."

But the words had barely left his mouth when his face twisted with discomfort. His breathing grew ragged, and a wave of nausea hit him hard— he doubled over in his seat.

Lori acted fast. She grabbed an airsickness bag and handed it to him just in time as he began to vomit. From a few rows away, Virgil had seen what was happening and was already making his way down the aisle.

A few seconds later, the man slumped back in his seat, visibly exhausted, though his face remained pale.

"I think I'm feeling better now… thank you," he murmured, offering a weak, embarrassed smile.

"Are you sure?" Lori asked, still not entirely convinced. Her instincts told her something wasn't quite right.

The man nodded, but Lori and Virgil exchanged a silent glance. Something felt off.

The passengers were beginning to show signs of fatigue, which was typical on long flights. Some were dozing in their seats, others got up to stretch their legs or use the restroom. Lori and her colleagues, as usual, kept their best smiles, working calmly, as if nothing were out of the ordinary. The looming threat of a possible bomb was still on their minds, but with each passing minute, it seemed more like a poorly timed joke than a real threat.

Lori, however, couldn't shake her sense of unease. She decided to approach the man who had handed her the envelope for the captain, hoping to catch something unusual in his behaviour. As she walked past, she noticed he was deeply asleep. But as she neared, the man stirred, his eyes opening with a curious glint.

"Excuse me…, did you give the envelope to the pilot?" he asked, his tone inquisitive but genuine. "Did the pilot say what it was about?"

Lori paused, meeting his gaze for a moment before answering, trying to keep her composure.

"No, he didn't say anything," she replied with a soft smile. "It was probably something personal. Don't worry about it."

The man nodded, seemingly satisfied with her response, and Lori walked away with a strange feeling in her chest. As she moved down the aisle, her mind raced, replaying the exchange. Later, she checked the passenger list and found nothing that suggested that the man was suspicious. His behaviour still seemed calm, even relaxed, as if everything were normal.

Despite the lingering sense of unease, Lori tried to relax. Perhaps it was all just a joke, a misunderstanding that would soon be forgotten. She allowed herself a deep breath, hoping to calm her nerves. In her mind, the words repeated like a mantra: Everything will be fine. There's no need to panic.

She thought about Jim and how he would react if he knew what was going on aboard the plane. It was better he didn't know, she decided. She didn't want to worry him, not today. And although the uncertainty still hung in the air, she clung to the hope that, in the end, everything would be alright.

Less than two hours before landing in Seattle, the tension in the cockpit was palpable. Captain Cummings and First Officer Monroe were maintaining constant communication with ground control, which had ordered a diversion from the flight path to fly over areas with low population density as a precautionary measure, in case the threat was real. Although they were still at 30,000 ft., the detour gave them time, but it also increased the uncertainty.

Cummings and Monroe exchanged glances, fully aware of what was at stake.

"We have a little over an hour left," Cummings said, adjusting the trajectory. "We need to buy time, but above all, we must stay calm. If the passengers start to notice anything strange, panic could break out, and that's the last thing we need."

"True, but if we start circling without descending, the passengers will notice," Monroe replied, concerned. "What will we tell them?"

Cummings paused, reflecting.

"The first thing is not to panic," he said. "We could tell them there's congestion in Seattle's air traffic and we're waiting for authorization to land. Something plausible to avoid raising suspicion."

Monroe nodded but still seemed worried.

"I understand. But what if someone starts asking too many questions?"

Cummings stood up and walked toward the cockpit door, looking at Monroe.

"I'll brief the crew," he said firmly. "Everyone needs to be in the loop, but without alarming the passengers."

With one last glance at the aircraft's indicators, Cummings opened the door and stepped out, determined to gather the flight attendants, and give them instructions on handling the situation with caution.

Once the team was assembled, the captain looked at them seriously, the weight of the situation hanging in the air.

"Listen carefully," Cummings began, his voice firm but with a slight edge of tension. "We've been instructed to divert toward less densely populated areas while we wait clearance to begin our descent into Seattle, which should happen shortly. The control tower has asked us to circle, descending cautiously while they prepare the runway for a possible emergency landing. But the most important thing now is to keep calm and manage everything with as much control as possible. The passengers can't notice anything.

Our priority is to make everything seem normal, even though we're dealing with a threat on board. Honestly, we don't know what's going to happen."

The flight attendants exchanged glances—tense, but resolute. They understood the gravity of the situation. It demanded precision, discretion, and above all, calm. Their mission was clear: maintain composure and prevent panic from spreading.

"For now, stick to your usual routines," Cummings instructed after a brief pause. "The last thing we need is for anyone to suspect something's wrong. We can't afford a panic."

They all nodded, fully aware of the stakes.

There was no room for mistakes.

"The situation is uncertain," Cummings went on, scanning each of their faces, his voice low and steady. "We're hoping it's a false alarm—but we have to be ready for the worst. Stay calm, stay in control. Prepare for a possible emergency landing, but for now, carry on as if everything is normal. The passengers must not suspect a thing. I'll make an announcement over the intercom shortly—stay sharp."

With that, he turned and headed back inside the cockpit, leaving the flight attendants to maintain the fragile illusion of normality. The tension was rising, but their training kicked in. Professionalism took over. They knew that everyone's safety depended on their ability to navigate the unknown with poise.

As the seatbelt signs lit up, the crew moved efficiently down the aisle, checking that passengers were seated and securing for landing. But someone had already noticed something was off.

"Excuse me, miss," said a passenger, leaning into the aisle. "Why did we change course? I've flown this route plenty of times—this isn't normal. And shouldn't we be descending by now?"

Lori, keeping her voice and her expression calm, responded smoothly:

"There's some heavy turbulence ahead, sir, so we've taken a different route to avoid it. Everything's under control. Please remain seated with your seatbelt fastened as a precaution."

The explanation seemed to settle him—temporarily. But the calm didn't last long.

Just then, the young man who had been feeling unwell earlier tried to stand and head toward the restroom. Without warning, he collapsed in the aisle.

Virgil, watching closely, reacted immediately. Rushing over, he and Lori managed to lift the man and guide him back to his seat. But now, the passenger was ghostly pale, drenched in sweat, and barely conscious—his condition sparking even deeper concern.

"Is there a doctor on board?" Lori called out; her voice urgent. The crew was trained in first aid, but this situation was clearly beyond basic procedures.

Fortunately, among the passengers was Frank, a paramedic travelling with his wife, Melinda, a nurse. The two immediately got up from their seats and quickly raised the armrests of the row to lay the young man down and assess him properly.

With his experience, Frank wasted no time in identifying the problem.

"This is a stage three appendicitis!—he needs surgery as soon as we land. Can you alert the pilot to have an ambulance waiting at Seattle Airport?" he said firmly, focusing on stabilizing the patient as best he could.

Lori, though trained for emergencies, froze for a moment. Her mind raced for the right response. How could she explain to Frank that landing wasn't an option right now—at least not without putting everyone else on board at risk?

Before she could say anything, Virgil stepped in with surprising calm.

"Yes, right away," he replied, giving Lori a look that clearly said, *let's not get into this now*. He knew they'd eventually have to tell the paramedic what was really going on, but now, wasn't the moment.

Without wasting a second, Virgil made his way to the cockpit to inform the captain of the new emergency. The tension in the cabin was thick. Although they were still following air traffic control's instructions—circling and descending gradually while waiting for clearance—the situation was becoming increasingly complicated.

Speaking into the interphone, Virgil said urgently, "Captain, it's Virgil. We've got another problem on board..."

Inside the cockpit, Cummings and Monroe exchanged a look. Things were spiralling out of control, and every second felt longer than the last. They were on the brink of a crisis that, although still uncertain in scope, would demand swift, decisive action.

Cummings quickly unlocked the cockpit door...

"Captain, we've got a passenger in critical condition. He needs immediate medical attention," Virgil said urgently as soon as he entered the cockpit, his voice tight with concern, eyes reflecting the weight of the situation. "We need to have an ambulance ready on the ground in Seattle."

"We'll alert ground control. Get back to your post, Virgil," Cummings replied with calm authority, his voice steady despite the tension mounting around them.

Monroe, acting swiftly, contacted the control tower in Seattle to ensure the ambulance would be standing by. The seriousness of the situation was clear—but what none of them knew was that worse might still be ahead.

Cummings paused for a moment, staring ahead into the dense clouds. A heavy silence filled the cockpit, broken only by the faint hum of instruments. The threat still looming aboard the plane had yet to reveal itself, and now the critical condition of a passenger only added more pressure to a situation already hanging by a thread.

A knot tightened in his stomach. He silently hoped they wouldn't need more ambulances… for anyone else who might be in danger in the moments to come. Things were unravelling fast. For a brief second, he closed his eyes and offered a silent prayer—that the threat looming around them was nothing more than a cruel joke.

He tried to picture the landing in Seattle as the end of the nightmare. But he knew every second counted. The burden of responsibility pressed down on him: the lives of the passengers, the crew, the decisions he still had to make. There was no room for error. No room for fear.

He drew a deep breath and steadied himself. Any sign of nerves could ripple through the cabin and trigger panic. Composed, he flipped on the intercom and spoke in a clear, confident voice:

"Good afternoon, ladies and gentlemen. This is your captain speaking. Some of you may have noticed we've slightly altered our course and have been in a holding pattern. This is due to congestion at Seattle's runways. We're currently waiting for clearance to land, so there may be a delay."

He paused, measuring his next words carefully.

"We'd also like to inform you that, due to a medical situation onboard, an ambulance will be waiting upon arrival to assist a passenger in need. We ask for your patience and cooperation, and please continue to follow the crew's instructions at all times. Thank you."

He clicked off the intercom and let out a long, slow breath. The delivery had to sound reassuring—

convincing. With luck, no one would question the real reason they were circling above the city.

As Monroe continued coordinating with the control tower, Cummings prepared for whatever might come next. He hoped it wouldn't require drastic action—but in case it did, he quietly said his goodbyes… to his wife… to his daughter… all in the silence of his mind.

Moments later, the response came through from the tower:

"Flight HA4925, begin slow descent."

"Roger that, control. Beginning descent to 26,000ft.," Monroe replied, his tone crisp and focused.

Cummings took the controls. Every mile lost brought them closer to the runway—and closer to the unknown. The cockpit was thick with tension, broken only by the crackle of the radio and the mechanical hum surrounding them.

Monroe's eyes remained locked on the instruments, monitoring every detail, while Cummings ran the procedures through his head again and again. Outside, dense clouds clung to the plane, casting the sky in a deep, disorienting grey.

With every metre they dropped, the weight of uncertainty grew heavier.

RUNWAY 16L

JUST BEFORE STARTING his shift, Jim poured himself a cup of coffee, savouring the warmth of the mug as a quiet smile spread across his lips. He was thinking about Lori. He was already counting down the hours until around 6:30 p.m.—the moment she'd have landed in Seattle and sent him her usual message, or maybe called with that sweet, comforting voice of hers that always arrived like clockwork. He knew, without a doubt, that she wouldn't let him down.

He pictured their conversation, the familiar rhythm of their little ritual. Sometimes, with a chuckle, they'd joke about "making love online." The thought made him smile again, a soft laugh escaping as he placed the mug back in the tray and adjusted his belt before heading out to patrol.

The first half of his shift unfolded like any other—patrolling the streets of Manhattan, assisting a distracted pedestrian, keeping a watchful eye on familiar trouble spots. But halfway through, a strange unease began to creep into his chest. There was no clear reason for it, just a tight, persistent knot that refused to go away.

He didn't have time to dwell on it.

The radio crackled to life with sudden urgency: a robbery in progress at a nearby bank. Instantly, Jim and Dimitri responded, racing toward the scene.

When they arrived, the red and blue strobes of patrol cars bathed the street in restless colour. Officers were already in position, weapons drawn, prepared for the worst. The SWAT team had breached the building from the rear and seemed to have the situation well in hand.

The suspect turned out to be a nervous young man, barely in his twenties, trying to pull off a heist like something out of a movie. But he quickly learned how far fiction was from reality. He surrendered without resistance, and the arrest was almost too easy. To everyone's surprise, his weapon turned out to be a plastic replica—realistic in appearance, but harmless.

Dimitri watched the handcuffed youth slumped on the sidewalk and shook his head, frustration furrowing his brow.

"This generation..." he muttered, arms crossed. "They'll do anything for attention. What did he think would happen? That we'd shoot him?" His tone carried anger, yes—but also something deeper. Concern. As the father of a twenty-two-year-old himself, he couldn't help but wonder what the hell these kids were wrestling with.

But Jim wasn't listening. His mind had already drifted. That tightness in his chest had returned, sharper now, more insistent. Like a warning. A premonition he couldn't explain, but couldn't ignore either.

The hours passed slowly as Dimitri and he went about their routine. Around six in the evening, he pulled out his phone and checked the screen. He knew it was still early for the call, but impatience led him to check anyway. He was eagerly waiting for it.

Nothing yet... of course!

At around 6:30, he checked again. Absolute silence. No missed calls, no messages, no trace of Lori.

But... there's still time.

By seven, unease settled heavier in his chest, growing with each passing minute. It wasn't like her to be late without letting him know. Even on the busiest days, she always found a moment to send a quick message, a confirmation that everything was fine.

He tried to calm himself. Maybe the flight had been delayed, or disembarking had taken longer than expected. These were logical, reasonable explanations, but they didn't quiet the feeling that something was wrong.

That call wasn't just part of a routine; it was their way of connecting across the distance, an anchor that kept them together. And now, the prolonged silence was starting to feel like something more than just a delay.

As night fell completely, Jim and Dimitri stopped next to the patrol car, each holding a steaming cup of coffee in their hands. The cool air carried the bitter aroma of the drink, though Jim barely noticed it.

Restless, he took another sip, barely tasting it, as his gaze shifted back and forth between his wristwatch and the phone screen, which remained stubbornly blank. No messages, no calls, no sign of Lori. The silence was starting to feel like an unbearable weight.

"Flights can sometimes be quite delayed, you know," Dimitri said calmly, noticing his friend checking the time every minute.

"But this much?" Jim replied, his voice tense. "What if something happened? Lori never gets late without letting me know. What if, actually…?" He fell silent, biting his lip, unwilling to finish the sentence.

The weight in his chest was becoming unbearable. With every passing minute, the feeling of distress grew into a thicker shadow, a silent warning that he couldn't ignore.

At exactly eight o'clock, he checked his watch again. No messages, no calls. Just an unsettling silence stretching on longer than it should have. Something was definitely wrong. He knew it with a chilling certainty. Deep down, in that corner of himself he rarely dared to visit, he felt it clearly.

They still had a couple of hours left in their shift. Sitting on the hood of the patrol car, they watched from a distance the café where they had bought their coffee just minutes before. Through the large windows, the TV screen flickered, though the sound didn't reach them. Distracted, Jim let his gaze wander across the scene, and suddenly something on the screen caught his attention. A familiar logo, Hawaiian Airlines, glowed on the display. In that instant, a chill ran through his body.

"That… that's related to something…" he murmured to himself, his mind already racing. Without thinking, he stood up and started walking quickly toward the café, with Dimitri following him, intrigued.

Inside, Jim rushed to the bar and asked the bartender to turn up the TV volume. Dimitri watched, still not fully understanding the urgency, but sensing that something wasn't right.

On the screen, the news anchor spoke in a serious tone:

> *"Apparently, Hawaiian Airlines flight HA4925, which departed New York at 11:30 this morning on route to Seattle, has yet to arrive… Reports suggest there may be an issue on board…"*

Jim's heart skipped a beat. He didn't need to hear more.

"That's Lori's flight!" he exclaimed, his voice cracking, unable to hide the panic that overwhelmed him.

Dimitri, shocked and unsure how to calm him, fell silent. The news on the TV continued, making the situation worse with every passing second.

"The problem is still unknown;
we are awaiting more details… We
will continue to update you…"

the anchor said, as the words fell like an unbearable weight on Jim.

He stood completely frozen, unable to move, his mind racing a thousand miles per hour, but his body glued to the ground, as if the air were compressing him. The anguish enveloped him like a cold, relentless cloak. He knew something was wrong, that unease, that strange feeling that had been haunting him all day… it had a reason. He had sensed it!

The happiness he had felt that morning, when he said goodbye to Lori, vanished in an instant, replaced by a palpable terror that overwhelmed him relentlessly. His mind screamed that something had happened to Lori, and he couldn't do anything to prevent it. He felt powerless and useless.

Dimitri, seeing the look of complete devasta-
tion on Jim's face, placed a hand on his shoulder, a simple gesture but one full of concern. However, neither the gesture nor the words seemed capable of calming the storm of emotions that was tearing through his friend.

"Jim, calm down, it's probably nothing serious. Maybe just a delay or a misunderstanding. Some turbulence, perhaps…" Dimitri tried to offer some comfort, but his voice sounded empty against the rising despair in Jim.

"Flight HA4925, descend to 23,000 feet," came the order from Seattle control, the voice crisp and steady through the radio.

"Roger, ground control," Cummings replied, his tone calm as his eyes flicked to the altimeter. The cockpit remained silent, save for the low hum of the engines and the rhythmic beeping of the instruments.

"We're running low on fuel…" he added quietly, his concern evident, though they still had enough to continue safely—for now.

The fuel gauge hovered near the limit. It wasn't yet critical, but it was close enough to make every second count. Cummings stayed sharp, scanning instruments, running calculations in his head, mentally preparing for any scenario.

They were already more than an hour behind schedule, delayed by the unexpected detour and the prolonged holding pattern. After circling for so long, the fuel reserves had taken a serious hit.

Back in the cabin, all appeared calm. Most passengers were unaware of the situation—aside from a few observant travellers who had noticed the odd flight path and repeated turns. But the captain's earlier announcement, casual yet reassuring, had eased most concerns. Trust held firm in the sound of authority.

Seatbelt signs remained lit, the official reason being turbulence. And indeed, the occasional bumps supported the claim, reinforcing the illusion of routine.

Meanwhile, in the cockpit, the descent continued—measured, precise, controlled.

"Twenty thousand feet…" Monroe murmured; eyes fixed on the altimeter.

"Nineteen," Cummings echoed, gaze locked ahead. Through shifting layers of clouds, the runway had begun to emerge—still distant, but now unmistakably visible, growing clearer with each passing second.

From the Seattle control tower, instructions continued to flow—clear, deliberate, and absolutely vital. Every word carried weight. The pilot knew that while the runway was drawing closer, there was no room for complacency. Everything had to go exactly right.

As the descent continued, the tension inside the cockpit thickened with each passing second.

"Thirteen thousand feet..." Monroe announced, holding his breath. His voice was tight, almost a whisper.

Cummings held his breath, eyes locked on the instruments. The control tower was still on the line, but even through the static, the tension was unmistakable. The air in the cockpit seemed denser now, heavy with anticipation—like any sound, even a breath, might tip the balance.

The altimeter ticked down: ...12,500 feet... No alarms. No warnings.

"Twelve thousand..." Monroe whispered, barely daring to say it out loud...

Cummings tightened his grip on the yoke. The silence pressed in on them, taut and expectant.

Then, for a fleeting second, their eyes met— and something passed between them. A glimmer of hope. They'd passed the ominous threshold of 13,000 feet... and still, all systems held steady.

"Nothing yet," Cummings said quietly, allowing himself the smallest exhale.

Monroe let out a dry, nervous chuckle. "Maybe..."

But a sudden jolt cut him off. The instrument panel flickered. A red warning light snapped on.

"Eleven-five," Monroe said, voice cracking under the strain.

Tension snapped back into the cockpit like a rubber band stretched too far. The radio was still live, but now even air traffic control had gone silent. Every soul on the frequency was holding their breath.

The plane, suspended between gravity and willpower, continued its descent...

In the passenger cabin, everything remained deceptively calm. Most travellers were unaware of the silent battle unfolding behind the cockpit door. But the crew—especially the veterans—felt it in their bones.

Flight attendants exchanged tense glances; lips pressed tight. Each shift in altitude stole their breath. Every faint vibration felt like a question they didn't dare ask aloud.

Virgil, the most experienced among them, glanced at his watch and then out the window. They had passed 13,000 feet... and nothing had happened.

He allowed himself a quiet moment of relief— but didn't let his guard down.

Subtly, he checked on his colleagues. A few gave the faintest nods. One pressed her lips together, eyes fixed ahead. Another crossed his fingers without thinking—an instinctive gesture of hope carefully hidden from passenger view.

Despite the apparent calm in the cabin, Lori knew they were not out of danger yet. Her training allowed her to maintain a serene expression, but with each passing second, she felt the weight of uncertainty.

An anxious passenger, her brow furrowed and her hands gripping the armrests, couldn't hide her discomfort at the prolonged descent. Her breathing was irregular, and her gaze nervously darted between the window and the aisle, as if searching for a sign that everything was under control. Finally, unable to contain her distress, she turned to Lori, who was walking down the aisle, making sure all passengers were okay. With a trembling voice, the woman asked her how much longer they would have to wait till touchdown.

Lori, mindful of the woman's fear of flying, gave her a warm smile, maintaining the serene composure she'd been trained to uphold. With a firm, reassuring tone, she replied:

"Not much longer, ma'am. We're almost there. Just a little more, and we'll be on the ground."

Her voice was an anchor amid the uncertainty. The passenger nodded, clinging to those words as if they were a promise, while the plane continued its descent.

Although Lori's words flowed naturally and her tone conveyed confidence, the anxiety inside her still simmered, burning like a contained flame.

For a moment, her mind escaped the cabin and flew to New York. She thought of Jim, his smile, the warmth of his voice at the end of the day. She wondered if he was feeling the same, if, in that very moment, his intuition was whispering to him that something was wrong.

She closed her eyes for a brief moment and, like a whisper to the wind, projected her thought toward him: *"I love you, Jim."*

Suddenly, a deafening roar shook the aircraft, ripping muffled screams and gasps of terror from the passengers. For an eternal moment, it seemed as though the plane would plummet immediately. And then, chaos!

A blast of icy wind violently burst into the cabin, swirling papers, tousling hair, and leaving behind a sharp whistle that echoed in their ears. The oxygen masks dropped suddenly, swinging like spectral pendulums. Some passengers, frozen by shock, took a moment to react; others, with trembling hands, hurriedly put them on, inhaling air desperately through the plastic. Although the altitude now allowed them to breathe without assistance, the sudden decompression had sown panic.

The plane pitched violently to the right and then to the left, shaking with such force that staying in their seats became nearly impossible. From the overhead compartments, which flew open with a deafening crash, suitcases, coats, and electronics rained down. A briefcase struck a man on the head, and he barely had time to raise his hands in defence.

Lori rushed toward him, gripping anything within reach to maintain her balance. Her priority was to check on him, ensuring he was unharmed. Thankfully, he only had a small bump on his head.

"It's nothing, I'm fine!" the man shouted, his voice barely audible above the deafening noise, struggling to be heard amid the chaos.

In the aisles, the flight attendants clung to anything stable, their voices barely rising above the din as they tried to issue instructions. Some passengers screamed in terror, others whispered frantic prayers, and a few remained frozen, their eyes wide and vacant, lost in their own panic.

In the cockpit, Captain Cummings and his co-pilot, Monroe, fought to control the plane.

Their screens flashed with red warnings, each more urgent than the last. The most alarming: a section of the cargo hold had exploded, leaving a gaping hole in the fuselage. Part of the luggage had been sucked into the void, taking with it any chance of deploying the landing gear.

"We're losing pressure!" Monroe shouted; his knuckles white as he gripped the throttle.

Cummings clenched his jaw. He knew they couldn't afford to lose their composure—not now.

"Emergency code!" he barked.

In the control tower, the explosion had already been logged. Operators scrambled over their monitors, desperately trying to locate the plane on radar.

"Flight HA4925, respond!" urged the air traffic controller, his voice firm, though tinged with rising panic.

A crackling burst of static. Then the captain's strained voice, barely coming through:

"This… flight… emergency…" The transmission abruptly cut out.

The silence that followed in the control tower was more chilling than any scream. They had lost the plane's location. Operators stared at their screens, frantic, as the signal seemed to evaporate into the void.

Suddenly, the central screen flickered, and the radio burst to life with static. They tried to spot it with the naked eye, but the distance made it nearly impossible. Darkness was beginning to fall, adding another layer of uncertainty to the scene.

Meanwhile, in the cockpit, Cummings struggled to maintain control of the plane. The fuel was almost depleted, and now all they had left was the hope of an emergency landing. Through the turbulence and the deafening roar of the air striking the fuselage, his eyes fixed on the horizon. In the distance, he spotted the lights of the city, and among them, he made out the runway, illuminated like a beacon in the darkness.

He remembered hearing the runway number before the communication with the control tower had been lost. "16L," that was all he had caught. Seeing that the runway was indeed glowing with intermittent red lights, he was able to distinguish it clearly. With no room for error, he aimed directly for it.

The plane descended almost steeply, its angle sharp from the speed. The passenger cabin shook with every violent movement. The passengers, growing paler by the second, struggled to remain in their seats, clinging to anything they could. Some already held motion sickness bags, their faces drenched in sweat, while the pressure on their stomachs intensified.

In the cockpit, Cummings and Monroe could see the runway. In the distance, they could make out emergency teams spreading foam over the tarmac, preparing for the worst. The engines roared loudly as Cummings and Monroe did their best to align the plane for a forced landing.

Meanwhile, inside the passenger cabin, Lori and the other flight attendants moved quickly, preparing the passengers for what they knew would be an emergency landing. Their voices were firm, though their own fear was evident in their eyes. They instructed the passengers to lean their heads forward, onto their knees, and to hold their legs with their arms. They reminded them not to undo their seatbelts and to keep their feet firmly on the floor. The tension was palpable, the air thick with collective fear.

Once all the passengers were prepared, the flight attendants took their positions, standing firm in their spots, positioned almost the same way as the passengers. At that moment, everyone knew that what happened next was beyond their control.

Jim's anxiety pushed him to drink more coffee than usual. While some people smoked when nervous, Jim turned to caffeine. Dimitri, watching in silence, warned him that too much coffee would only fuel his anxiety, but Jim didn't seem to hear. Dimitri understood all too well what was consuming his friend—he could see the worry gripping him—but he couldn't help noticing how Jim's mind was trapped in a spiral of uncertainty.

They still had two hours of patrol left, but Jim couldn't focus on anything other than the news about Lori's flight. Dimitri, knowing his friend's restless nature, suggested he try to stop thinking about it. But he knew it was an almost impossible task—asking Jim to stop thinking about Lori was like asking him to stop breathing.

Unless they got an emergency alert, their only mission was clear: stay at the café, eyes glued to the TV. The news continued to churn out updates about the emergency landing of flight HA4925. Jim's eyes were fixed on the screen, barely blinking, terrified of missing any crucial piece of information.

Dimitri, ever the pragmatic, tried to reassure him. If anything came up at the station, he'd handle it, understanding the extraordinary circumstances. He was sure they'd understand. But even as he spoke, the tension in the air was thick, palpable. Jim wasn't hearing him—his mind kept circling back to the same question: *How is Lori?*

So, they sat in silence, listening to each new update, torn between anxiety and hope, clinging to the belief that this wouldn't end in tragedy. Jim had no intention of leaving until he knew for sure—until he knew that Lori had landed safely.

The airport fire trucks, along with the ambulances, sped down the runway toward the emergency landing site. From the distance, they watched as flight HA4925 approached dangerously.

Just before touching down, Cummings, with his hands firmly on the controls, gently raised the plane's nose, braking decisively and trying to keep the aircraft straight as it slid over the foam covering the runway. The impact when it hit the ground was brutal, a hard jolt that resonated through the fuselage. The plane continued sliding, skidding against the asphalt, sparks flying around it. The thick foam layer and the fact that the fuel was nearly exhausted prevented a fire from breaking out, though the fuselage sustained severe damage during the braking process, with pieces of the belly tearing off as the plane sped down the runway.

The runway was nearly finished when, finally, the plane came to a complete stop, just a few meters from the end.

Inside the plane, the chaos of evacuation began immediately. The flight attendants quickly moved to the emergency exits, where the slides deployed without issues. Lori and her colleagues gave clear instructions: leave personal belongings behind, remove shoes quickly, and evacuate without delay but calmly. They assisted and guided passengers to the exits, ensuring they left the aircraft in an orderly fashion. Some of the attendants had already slid down the ramps to help passengers once they reached the ground.

Ambulances, fire trucks, and rescue teams were ready to intervene. One by one, passengers began descending the slides. The first to go down was the man with appendicitis, evacuated along with the paramedic and his wife. Fortunately, all other passengers emerged unscathed, except for a few scratches and bruises. The crew, though battered, also managed to evacuate without major issues. The last to leave were the crew members, ensuring that all passengers were safely off the plane.

A crown of journalists had filtered onto the runway to get closer to the accident site and broadcast the situation live.

Once off the plane, all passengers and crew were transported by bus to the terminal, where they underwent medical checks before being cleared to leave. They were then taken to the waiting area, where they could retrieve their belongings left inside the plane, as well as some items recovered from the cargo hold that hadn't been thrown out or lost.

After the medical check-up, the entire crew, including Cummings and Monroe, gathered to have something warm to drink. Some, seeking comfort, opted for a stronger drink, trying to calm their nerves and dissipate the tension that still lingered. Grateful that everything had gone well, they sat together, surrounded by a deep sense of camaraderie, leaving behind the chaos and uncertainty of the terrifying experience. The feeling of relief brought them even closer, as if the weight of the ordeal was lifting with each word and every shared gesture.

It was in those moments of relaxation and relief that some took the opportunity to call their families. Lori, relieved, didn't hesitate to pull out her phone and, without much thought, dialled Jim's number.

Jim remained at the café, trapped in uncertainty, until the television announced that all passengers and crew on flight HA4925 had been rescued without any fatalities or serious injuries. A deep sight of relief escaped his lips. Then, amidst the images being broadcast, he thought he saw Lori in the distance, helping the passengers. She appeared unharmed. His heart, which had been gripped by anxiety, now swelled with happiness.

It was 9:20 p.m. in New York when the sound of his phone broke the silence. Jim's heart raced as he looked at the screen and saw Lori's name. A mixture of excitement and fear gripped him as he answered immediately. A lump formed in his throat, making it hard to speak.

"Darling…" Jim whispered, his voice barely audible, thick with the emotion he'd been holding back.

"I saw you on the news… Are you okay, my love?"

"Jim, my love, I'm fine… I just need to see you," Lori replied, her eyes welling up with happy tears. "For a moment, I thought I'd never see you again… Everything happened so fast, so suddenly… But it's over now. It's all behind us." She tried to downplay it, though her voice still trembled with emotion. "I'll tell you everything when we see each other, darling. What an adventure!"

They both laughed and cried, all at the same time, overwhelmed by relief at having made it through the most terrifying moment.

"What a scare! But now I can breathe easy, my love. I'm almost done with my shift, and I'll finally sleep peacefully knowing I'll see you soon." Jim laughed nervously, still trying to process everything that had happened. "You must've been terrified, darling. You must be exhausted. I guess they'll take you to the hotel now…"

"Yes… scared of never seeing you again, sweetheart. But now we're celebrating our rescue, our lives, the whole crew… Everything turned out okay." Lori sighed with relief. "They'll take us to the hotel soon, and we can finally rest. I'm counting the hours until I see you Thursday morning when I arrive, my love."

"I love you so much, sweetheart…" Jim whispered, his heart in his throat. "I can't wait to see you again… and to make you, my wife."

"And I, darling. But Thursday is almost here, and we'll be together soon. Sweet dreams, honey."

"Rest well, beautiful." Jim said, unable to hide the smile spreading across his face.

They ended the call with a kiss, a gesture that didn't go unnoticed by Lori's colleagues, who cheered in delight.

Jim, hearing the noise, couldn't help but ask, laughing, sensing something.

"What's going on over there?"

Lori, blushing slightly, replied through her laughter.

"It's my colleagues; they're applauding our virtual kiss…"

Jim laughed warmly before saying goodbye: "Goodbye, my love. Rest well… I love you."

His voice was full of relief and happiness.

"You too, honey. I'll see you Thursday morning. I love you too." After one final kiss over the phone, they hung up.

Shortly after, the transport that would take the crew to the hotel arrived.

As the vehicle approached, a wave of relief washed over the group, followed by spontaneous applause. The applause not only celebrated the end of an exhausting and unforgettable day, but also the sheer fortune of having come through such a terrifying experience unscathed.

Some laughed nervously, still processing what had happened, while others closed their eyes, succumbing to the fatigue. The tension began to dissolve, replaced by a sense of gratitude and calm. Finally, they could rest.

Lori had one last flight back the following day, Wednesday. The departure was scheduled for 9:50 p.m. from Seattle, with an expected arrival in New York at 6:00 a.m. on Thursday, local time. Despite her exhaustion, the thought of returning home and being reunited with Jim gave her the strength to face one last day in the air.

In the wake of the incident, the FBI launched a thorough investigation to determine who had placed the bomb on the aircraft and how they had managed to bypass security protocols. Despite the agents' best effort, the investigation was still ongoing, and every new lead uncovered seemed to raise more questions than answers...

¡MERRY CHRISTMAS!

Lori had flight HA6744 scheduled to depart at 9:50 p.m. from Seattle (SEA), local time, with an arrival in New York (JFK) at 6:00 a.m., New York time. This would be her last flight before her wedding. That Thursday not only marked the end of her workday but also the start of her wedding and honeymoon holidays. Lori and Jim would have a fortnight all to themselves, a time free of worries, just to enjoy their most awaited moment: their wedding and the honeymoon that would follow.

When Lori arrived in New York, Jim was already waiting for her with a huge bouquet of flowers in hand, at the exit of the baggage claim area.

The romantic spectacle was set. They embraced with such intensity it felt like time stopped, sealing the moment with a passionate kiss that made the other travellers and crew members feel envious. Jim, unable to wait a second longer, picked her up in his arms as if they were crossing the threshold of their new life together. He carried her to the car, while the crowd applauded their charming gesture.

Lori laughed, both happy and a little embarrassed, aware that they were the centre of everyone's attention. But no matter what others thought, that moment belonged only to them.

They didn't have the traditional bachelor or bachelorette parties, but they had made it their own—on the go! Between Lori's flight breaks, they shopped for and tried on their wedding outfits, with the help of her twin sister Lily and Jim's sister Nicky, who were by her side every step of the way. Along the journey, they pulled together a small, intimate celebration—including their moms, who were just as excited to join the fun!

Amidst the festive, Christmas-filled atmosphere of the city, they hopped from café to pub, enjoying drinks and laughter, creating their own version of a bachelorette party. While it wasn't the typical loud and boisterous celebration, it was enough for them. A moment of joy, love, and camaraderie.

Meanwhile, Dimitri, along with Andy, Jim's younger brother, and some fellow police officers, had organized their own version of a bachelor party for Jim. After their shifts, they gathered for a few beers and jokes among friends. A camaraderie-filled moment that marked the end of his bachelorhood.

However, the true bachelor and bachelorette party was one Lori and Jim had together, in their own way, without following any conventions. They snuck away for a romantic dinner, enjoyed a carriage ride through Central Park, and let themselves be enveloped by the magic of the Christmas lights illuminating the city. It was a more personal, intimate farewell. Jim continued to play the game of winning her over once more, while she pretended to be indifferent, though their smiles and gazes betrayed the excitement they shared.

Finally, they ended their special day in an elegant hotel suite, where, surrounded by luxury and romance, they consummated their love… and with it, the end of their singlehood. A day that would be etched in their hearts, marking the beginning of a new chapter together.

The following day, Friday, was Christmas Eve, and both the O'Hara and Kiloha families gathered to celebrate it together. The party was held at Jim's parent's house, where a splendid Christmas dinner was prepared, with the traditional turkey, puddings, and, of course, the delicious and charming gingerbread cookies in the shape of little men, which everyone eagerly awaited. The atmosphere was relaxed and familial; there was no need to dress formally, but comfortably, so nearly everyone chose sweaters, cardigans, or shirts with Christmas patterns, a tradition of the O'Hara family that added a festive and fun touch to the gathering.

The living room glowed with the twinkle of lights wrapped around a towering, glittering Christmas tree. Its shiny ornaments scattering reflections across the room. Beneath the tree, a generous pile of gifts waited—one for everyone, whether they'd been good… or even a little bit naughty. Why not? It's Christmas, after all! In the end, no one would leave without a gift.

The hosts, Conor and Selena—Jim's parents— were joined by their children: Andy, the youngest of the O'Hara siblings; Nicky, the middle child; and, of course, Jim himself.

The honoured guests, the Kiloha family, included Vincent and Gwendolyn—Lori's parents, who had travelled from Hawaii for the wedding. They were joined by Lori's twin sister, Lily, and Lori herself, of course, to share this special evening.

Though it wasn't a large crowd, the celebration was warm and heartfelt, evoking the traditional Christmases of the past. Each person contributed something special to the event: a bottle of wine, some champagne, fresh flowers, typical holiday sweets, and Gwen prepared some Hawaiian treats, while Vince made his homemade Hawaiian punch with love.

Before dinner, everyone held hands around the table in a gesture of unity and gratitude. They prayed and gave thanks for the blessings received during the year, for Lori's safe return home, for the delicious meal prepared with such care, and for the future husband and wife, whose union would be celebrated the next day, as well as for the families now intertwined.

They sang Christmas carols, played family games, and laughed at jokes—some of them quite bad—that the kids kept telling. The laughter, filled with affection, filled the house, while the lights on the tree blinked softly.

For Jim and Lori, this Christmas was even more special, as it was the first they shared together, surrounded by their loved ones. The warmth of the night, the love of their families, and the simple act of being together created a magical atmosphere.

When it was time to say goodbye, Jim and Lori knew they wouldn't see each other again until the afternoon of the following day, Christmas Day... the day of their wedding. Everything was ready, and they were excited... and nervous, too! They felt as though they were about to begin a new chapter in their lives, and the anticipation surrounded them with a mix of happiness and excitement.

In one year, they promised, Christmas would be celebrated in their own home, as husband and wife. And no one present could miss it... under threat of being disinherited from the punch and cookies!

The big day arrived: Christmas Day. Everyone was expecting snow, but the surprise was that, instead of a morning snowfall, the snow arrived right at the end of the celebration, when the party was at its peak. As Lori and Jim departed for their honeymoon, the snow began to fall gently, like a special gift to seal that unique moment.

Lori's wedding dress was a big secret, known only by Gwen, her mother, Lily, her twin sister, and, of course, herself. Not even Vince, her father, had any idea what it would look like. The emotion on his face when he saw her in the dress would be indescribable.

Following tradition, Lori wore something old: her shoes, elegant and comfortable white heels she had worn on other occasions, which, unlike new ones, wouldn't cause her any discomfort. Something new, of course, was her dazzling wedding dress. The borrowed item was her paternal grandmother's earrings, Leilani Kiloha, a beautiful symbol of the connection to her family and the heritage she carried in her heart. And, finally, something blue: the garter, which not only fulfilled the tradition but would also become a fun and memorable moment during the party.

Her maid of honour would be her twin sister, Lily, who had always been by her side, and as a bridesmaid, Nicky, Jim's sister, who supported her as if she were her own sister. Everything was set to make this day one to remember, full of love, laughter, and plenty of emotion.

As for the groom, Jim had never felt more nervous. Dressed in a timeless black tuxedo—a classic that never goes out of style—he wore it with his usual quiet elegance, pairing it with an immaculate black bow tie. Standing proudly by his side as his best man, was his younger brother, Andy. He wore a red bow tie, a slight variation that set him apart, because he believed the groom should be the one to stand out.

Dimitri, of course, would also be present, as one of the groomsmen, though, as expected, he wouldn't show up in any photo. He couldn't stand being the centre of attention, especially in front of a camera! While his presence and support were deeply appreciated, he was happiest staying behind the scenes, enjoying the celebration without being caught on film.

But…

Instead of just telling you about the wedding and all its details, why not enjoy it in person?

Please read on…

Dear reader…

Jim and Lori would be delighted to have the honour of your presence at their wedding—a day filled with love, laughter, and the kind of joy that lingers long after the last dance.

You are cordially invited, not just as a guest, but as someone who has walked beside them through every twist, turn, and tender moment.

Come as you are, with your heart full and your spirit light.

Come and enjoy a glass of champagne, and toast for the newlyweds!

But that's not all... you'll also have the chance to meet the author of this story, that is, me , and enjoy a performance of the unique and endearing characters who bring this romance to life.

It will be an event you won't want to miss!

And all you have to do is scan this QR!

Hope you enjoy it!